"Have you ever allowed yourself to get really close to anyone?"

"N-not...that close, no."

"A real loner," he commented. "And thus—a virgin, no doubt."

"You say it as if it's some sort of unpleasant disease."

"Not at all. Just a crying shame," he murmured, and his gaze lingered on her bare arms, the smooth curve of her throat, her hair. "Well, should we try dessert?"

"You can't simply say things like that and expect to get away with it!"

"What did you have in mind?"

LINDSAY ARMSTRONG married an accountant from New Zealand and settled down—if you can call it that—in Australia. A coast-to-coast camping trip later, they moved to a six-hundred-acre mixed-grain property, which they eventually abandoned to the mice and leeches and blackflies. Then, after a winning career at the track with an untried trotter, purchased "mainly because he had blue eyes," they opted for a more conventional family life with their five children in Brisbane, where Lindsay now writes.

Books by Lindsay Armstrong

HARLEQUIN PRESENTS PLUS
1656—UNWILLING MISTRESS

HARLEQUIN PRESENTS
1487—LEAVE LOVE ALONE
1546—A DANGEROUS LOVER
1569—DARK CAPTOR
1593—AN UNUSUAL AFFAIR
1626—THE SEDUCTION STAKES

HARLEQUIN ROMANCE
2653—DON'T CALL IT LOVE
2785—SOME SAY LOVE
2876—THE HEART OF THE MATTER
2893—WHEN THE NIGHT GROWS COLD
3013—THE MARRYING GAME

LINDSAY ARMSTRONG

A Difficult Man

Harlequin Books

TORONTO • NEW YORK • LONDON
AMSTERDAM • PARIS • SYDNEY • HAMBURG
STOCKHOLM • ATHENS • TOKYO • MILAN
MADRID • WARSAW • BUDAPEST • AUCKLAND

ISBN 0-373-11693-4

A DIFFICULT MAN

CHAPTER ONE

'WHO the hell are you?'

Juanita Spencer-Hill stared dazedly at the tall, violently irritated-looking man who had flung open the door she'd just knocked politely upon. She'd seen Gareth Walker interviewed on television on the subject of his latest bestseller and had been, to an extent, prepared for some sort of impact. There'd been little doubt he'd come across through the small screen as sharply, almost annihilatingly intelligent and dynamic and had then projected the laid-back charm of a man who was both worldly and considerably experienced with women—to the discomfort of his interviewer, a lady renowned for her cool, unflappable manner. And it had annoyed Juanita that he should be able to do that, and not only that—probably have the millions of women watching him wonder wistfully what he'd be like to go to bed with, as well. But in the flesh and despite his palpable irritation the impact was doubled. His dark blond hair was thick and straight, his eyes the deepest blue she'd ever seen. His physique was commanding despite a scruffy khaki shirt and faded jeans—it was powerful yet with not an ounce of superfluous weight and he was well over six feet . . .

'I repeat,' Gareth Walker said through his teeth, 'who the hell are you? And why are you standing there gawking at me?'

Juanita closed her mouth and flushed. 'I'm not,' she said curtly, and held out her hand. 'I'm Juanita S-

Spencer-Hill from Bluemoon Interiors and it was arranged that I arrive here at precisely this time to——'

'*Spencer*-Hill,' he interrupted, and continued without so much as an apology, 'I thought they were sending me a plain Miss Hill.' He ignored her outstretched hand although he stared at it for a moment, at her long, slim fingers adorned only by a gold signet-ring on the little finger, at her fragile wrist and large gold watch with its black velvet band and the delicate gold-link bracelet she wore with it. Then he raised those remarkable blue eyes and proceeded to scan her from head to toe with an insolent kind of thoroughness. From her glossy dark hair tied back in the nape of her neck, her dark eyes, her tall, slender figure in a beautifully cut black and white Liberty-print dress with its long skirt, to her flat black shoes, and then to her walking stick. What he made of it she was not to know immediately because as their gazes locked again he said sardonically, 'Speak up, ma'am. I'm all agog.'

Juanita bit her lip and blushed again. 'M-my mistake, Mr Walker. I work under the name of Hill but it s-slipped my mind.'

'Now why would you go around deceiving people like that, I wonder, Miss Spencer-Hill?' he said then. 'When it doesn't slip your mind.' He raised a mocking eyebrow at her.

Juanita gathered her wits. 'I don't see it as a deception,' she said coolly. 'I——'

'Well, I do. I assume you are one of *those* Spencer-Hills? The flamboyant family that boasts a star of the silver screen, an Archibald prize-winner and a budding Juan Fangio?'

Juanita winced and wondered what she'd done to deserve this. 'M-my father is an actor, my mother a portrait painter and my brother drives Formula One cars, and it's merely because I don't like to trade on their reputations that I—w-work under another name——'

'Or that you'd like to dissociate yourself from them?' he broke in with a cutting little smile.

Juanita took a breath and said grimly, 'I don't propose to discuss my family any further with you, Mr Walker, nor to stand here and be insulted any longer. I came on business but it would appear you've taken an instantaneous dislike to me which would make that business impossible to transact, so I'll leave. Good-day.'

She started to turn away but he said softly, '*Bravo*! You didn't stammer once. Why do you use a walking stick?'

'I—it's none of your——'

'Business?' he offered with a lightning grin and change of mood that bewildered her. 'OK. Let's revert to what is my business—— Well, come in.' He stood aside then put his head to one side with a frown. 'How old are you, Miss Spencer-Hill?'

Juanita stared at him. 'That's none of your business either,' she said stiffly.

'Oh, I think it is,' he said blandly. 'You *are* here to redecorate my house from top to bottom so we need to know *something* about each other. I'm thirty-six, incidentally,' he added obligingly. 'Whereas you look to be about . . . twenty-eight?'

'I'm twenty-five,' Juanita said flatly before she could stop herself.

'Damn!' He grimaced. 'If there's one sure way to offend a woman it's to overestimate her age. What can I do to make amends?'

'Nothing. My being a woman is entirely irrelevant——'

'I beg to differ. One's sex can never be irrelevant despite what radical feminists like to think—are you one of those, Miss Spencer-Hill?' he enquired curiously but with his blue eyes laughing at her.

'Not at all,' she denied frigidly.

'Good. On two counts—I can't stand 'em and I wouldn't have believed you if you'd claimed to be one anyway. But why are we discussing this standing on the doorstep? Do come in, Miss Spencer-Hill. My study is just across the hall. We can continue this riveting conversation there in much more comfort,' he said gravely and turned to lead the way.

Juanita glared at his back but after a moment followed. It was, after all, she reminded herself, her first major assignment.

'There. Comfortable?' Gareth Walker queried as he lounged back behind a beautiful walnut desk and studied the way she sat, upright and with her hands in her lap, opposite him. 'My apologies for welcoming you so ungraciously,' he added. 'I'd forgotten you were coming. I'd also been seized by inspiration this morning—did you know I was a writer?'

'Yes——'

'Then you'll probably be able to forgive my emotional excesses. Particularly as you have an artist in the family. How is your dear mother, by the way? I've met her several times.'

'She's very well, thank you,' Juanita replied. 'Mr Walker——'

'Is your parents' famous open marriage still as open as it used to be?'

Juanita set her lips and merely stared at him.

'I've always thought,' he went on, undeterred, 'that one's children suffer most in those kind of irregular arrangements. Is that why you have a slight speech impediment, Miss Spencer-Hill?'

Juanita paled as this unerring dart struck home. But she said with tight-lipped precision, 'Even as a generalisation that sounds pretty glib but as an invasion of someone's privacy it's intolerable. What——' she looked down at her hands then up at him '—m-makes you think you have the right to subject *anyone* to this kind of inquisition, Mr Walker?'

He took his time answering. He appeared to be giving it serious consideration in fact but all the while he was studying her critically so that she started to feel uncomfortable in a different way.

He said at last, 'I can't bear beating about the bush. Can you?'

Whatever she'd expected it wasn't this. She blinked, causing him to smile absently. 'I . . . n-no,' she said. 'All the same—well, it's not the same thing anyway,' she finished exasperatedly.

He sat up. 'I think it is. Look at it this way, which is the more practical way of doing things—for me to wonder why you have a stammer and need a walking stick but be too polite to ask, even try to avoid the subject and make myself uncomfortable and no doubt put my foot in it from time to time—or for you to tell me and thus get it all out of the way so that we can go forward and do—er—business?'

'It's *still* not the same thing,' Juanita protested. 'You've insulted my parents——'

'Well, that too is better got out of the way—I mean, forgive me, but I'm sure one of the reasons you've chopped your name in half is to escape the inevitable curiosity people have about them. They are such a—high-profile couple, aren't they?'

Juanita returned his suddenly direct, probing gaze in silence for about a minute. Then she said drily, 'I have a feeling about you, Mr Walker.'

He raised an amused eyebrow. 'In what respect, Miss Spencer-Hill?'

'That you have a talent for getting your own way and are——'

'What made you think that?'

'Would you please stop interrupting me?'

'Very well.' He composed his features into an expression of polite interest.

Juanita gritted her teeth. 'You must project that aura, Mr Walker,' she said tartly. 'But to get back to *your* incredible curiosity, for want of a kinder term, my parents are both very talented individuals and...some of the things they've done are because of the way they're made; in other words they haven't been able to help themselves, but I love them both. After all, you, no doubt, put your extreme insensitivity and the emotional excesses you mentioned earlier down to the way *you're* made,' she said with unmistakable satire.

'Go on.'

She thought for a moment, then continued steadily, 'I should add that I'm only telling you these things because, not to mention discomfiting *you*——' her dark eyes glinted '—losing your account could put a bit of a blight on *my* career... I had a car accident. I'm almost fully recovered but my left hip can be weak under strain and I've always stammered. Could we get to work now, do you think?' she queried crisply.

He stared at her steadily then pushed his chair back and stood up. 'By all means. I'm sure you'll feel much better with all that out in the open. Where would you like to start—are you staying the night?'

'Several nights was the——' Juanita stopped and bit her lip.

'Why not? An excellent idea!' Gareth Walker came round the front of the desk and leant against it with his arms folded, his eyes sparkling with mocking amusement.

Juanita compressed her lips. 'It wasn't *my* idea,' she said. 'I mean,' she amended, 'the alternative was that I stay in a nearby motel but I believe you——'

'So I did,' he broke in blandly, then grimaced. 'I'm quite absent-minded about a lot of things but at the time it didn't seem practical to have motel expenses added to the cost when you could lose ten people in this house without noticing it. I do also now remember telling them that I'd put up with whatever it takes, provided they *didn't* drag it out too long.'

'I'll certainly do my best to keep it to the minimum,' Juanita said wearily. 'But of course you might not like my ideas at all. This is what this first visit is about. For me to produce some preliminary sketches and ideas.'

He grimaced. 'You look as if the mere thought of it is like scaling Mount Everest. I wonder why?'

'I can tell you. Decorating houses is no problem, Mr Walker. It's their owners who often are.'

He laughed outright. 'Well said, Miss Spencer-Hill! I admire your candour. I admire other things about you as well,' he added. 'Has your mother ever painted you?'

Juanita's eyes widened in some confusion. 'No,' she said slowly. 'Why should she?'

'Come now,' he said with irony. 'You must know you're rather remarkable.'

'I d-don't,' Juanita disagreed. 'I'm tall and thin, I have the kind of skin that easily looks sallow, I m-might always limp and stammer——' She stopped abruptly.

'You also have wonderful hair and eyes and all your skin needs is a bit of sun to make it look like warm ivory; you're not *that* thin,' he said, his gaze resting squarely on her breasts beneath the closely fitted dress, 'and with a waist as slim as yours you'd look top-heavy any other way; but beside all that, you have an air of elegance— and an air of tantalising mystery and reserve. I can't believe no man has made this known to you, Miss Spencer-Hill.'

Juanita couldn't help the colour that came to her cheeks. 'N-not really—I mean——'

'That's another thing,' he went on. 'Do you know that you stammer when you're nervous? When you're angry you're quite fluent. But I'm puzzled as to why being complimented should make you nervous.'

I'm imagining this, Juanita thought. Is he making a pass or—what?

'No, I'm not. Yet,' Gareth Walker said softly.

'H-how did you know...?'

His lips twisted. 'Your expression.'

Juanita bit her lip, then frowned. 'Yet? What does that mean?'

'Just that——'

'Now look here, Mr Walker——'

'Do call me Gareth,' he said pleasantly.

'No. I shall do no such thing——'

'There's nothing compromising in it these days.'

Juanita closed her lips tightly and glared at him.

'What does *that* mean?' he parodied.

'It means that I really don't think we can work together, Mr Walker. For one thing I can never get a word in edgeways. For another...' She shrugged.

He waited, with his arms folded, his blue eyes glinting wickedly until she said exasperatedly, 'What now?'

'I was just allowing you to finish what you were going to say,' he murmured. 'For another reason...?'

'It doesn't matter,' Juanita said shortly.

'I thought it might have something to do with what was going through your mind earlier. The dread possibility that I might be trying to—er—chat you up.'

'All right, yes,' she conceded coldly. 'I certainly couldn't work with anyone under those conditions.'

He raised an eyebrow. 'What conditions?'

'I should have thought that was obvious!'

'It's not. I mean, it would be with someone who made a habit of chatting up girls, but I don't.'

Juanita breathed heavily. 'I only have your word for it. *You* were the one who brought the subject up, after all.'

'No, you were the one who *thought* it,' he replied. 'I merely made it known to you that I thought you were an interesting, in some ways arresting woman on first impressions—I hadn't got much further in my deductions as a matter of fact, which was why I uttered that fatal little word—*yet*—whereupon you immediately became deeply suspicious and got on your high horse. But, if this sets your mind at rest, Miss Spencer-Hill, I make it a habit to get to know persons of the opposite sex much better than we know each other before I like to become intimate with them.'

Juanita stared at him angrily and incredulously.

'Are you lost for words?' he queried, his eyes mocking her again. 'If so, may I——?'

'No, you may not.' The words came at last. 'I'm not going to play this ridiculous game of semantics with you any longer. What's more, should your deductions lead you at any future date to feel that I'm worthy of becoming intimate with, don't waste your time.'

'Why?'

'Why *what*?'

'Why are you so automatically discounting the possibility that once we got to know each other we might both like and admire one another?'

'Because I don't go around thinking about those things all the time and especially not when I'm on a business assignment,' she stated coolly.

'What does it take to make you think of them, then?'

'Well, it would appear obvious that *you* don't, Mr Walker,' Juanita said blandly. 'May we *please* proceed?'

'Certainly,' he said with a faint, imperturbable smile. 'Do you never have qualms about things like famous last words?'

Juanita stood up abruptly, which was a mistake, as her hip let her know, and she stumbled slightly at the same time as she fumbled for her stick.

'Here.' He put his hands on her waist, steadied her briefly then withdrew them and handed her the stick.

'Thank you,' she said tautly, and stopped. There was only a couple of inches between them and as her eyes met his she found she couldn't help but be supremely conscious of it, and him.

I don't believe it, she thought, appalled. Yet disbelief was no shield for the heat that came to her skin, and not only to her cheeks but all over as his gaze, which betrayed no more than a grave thoughtfulness with just a tinge of irony, returned hers. Nor did it alleviate the curious stirring of her pulses as he simply waited—and watched.

It did occur to her that, as had happened to the lady interviewer, it was not that easy to remain unaffected by Gareth Walker despite a revulsion towards the concept that some men just had that kind of impact on women and he was one of them, and not unlike her excessively good-looking father so far as that kind of thing went. It also occurred to her, and was no comfort, that he'd behaved abrasively, even outrageously towards *her*, so she had less excuse for being caught like a girl in this kind of trap. But the fact was that she was arbitrarily, and unfairly, quite unable to draw her mind or her gaze from the width of his shoulders beneath his khaki shirt, his disordered hair lying on his forehead, his hands and the memory of how they'd felt on her waist . . .

It had never happened to her before. Not this purely physical sense of curiosity and this new concept of the unspoken channels of communication between a man and a woman—the speaking of the senses, she thought a little wildly. How does he do it? More importantly, why is he doing it to me? Or is it second nature or——?

A knock on the door caused her to start convulsively and him to grimace faintly before he turned his head and said, 'Come in!'

It was a girl of no more than nineteen who stepped into the study saying, 'Gareth? Do you know someone's here? But I can't find them—oh! Sorry. So *you* must be the owner of that neat little BMW outside. Good-day! I'm Wendy, the housekeeper.'

She couldn't have looked less like a housekeeper if she'd tried, Juanita thought, in her blue jeans, pink shirt and blonde pony-tail with a pink ribbon.

'Apprentice housekeeper, filling in for her mother who is ill at present,' Gareth Walker said wryly. 'Wendy, this is Miss Spencer-Hill, the interior decorator I—forgot to tell you about.' He grimaced. 'She'll be staying a couple of days—well, she'll be popping in and out on and off for quite some weeks, I gather.'

'Forgot!' Wendy wrinkled her brow and clicked her tongue. Then she brightened. 'So you are going to get it done. That's super! Mum will be really pleased with you.'

'I'm so glad,' Gareth said with not a flicker of a smile and turned to Juanita. 'Wendy's mother is our regular housekeeper and she rules us with a rod of iron but she's in hospital so Wendy's holding the fort. Where——' he turned back to the girl '—do you imagine your unmentionable siblings are? I haven't heard them all morning.'

It was at that moment that the sounds of a shrill, urgent and acrimonious squabble made themselves heard, causing them all to glance simultaneously towards the window which overlooked the gravelled forecourt with its pond and fountain. Juanita's eyes widened as she saw two children of about seven engaged in what appeared to be deadly, hair-pulling, punching, kicking and scratching combat.

'If,' Wendy said wearily, 'you're talking about my brother and sister, that's them. I'll——'

'No, I will,' Gareth Walker said drily. 'You take Miss Spencer-Hill to a guest bedroom and——' he glanced at his watch '—perhaps we could all meet again for lunch?'

Wendy chattered non-stop as she led the way towards a guest bedroom. 'I always keep one made up just in *case*,' she said cheerfully. 'You can never tell with Gareth. Isn't it exciting? I'd love to have your job but I suppose it takes an awful lot of training—here we are—but you haven't got a suitcase or anything!'

Juanita grimaced. 'I left it in the car. I thought I'd make myself known first and then I forgot about it——'

'I'll get it for you!'

'Oh, you don't have to do that, Wendy. I can——'

'No, I will—you're limping anyway. I must say, Miss Spencer-Hill——' Wendy looked at her admiringly '—I'd *love* to look as elegant as you do but I never seem to get it right. Gareth says not to worry, he can't stand elegant women who look as if they've stepped out of a fashion magazine, but men don't understand these things, do they? Now you sit down and rest your poor leg,' she said kindly, adding, 'Did you sprain your ankle or something?'

'It's my hip,' Juanita murmured and did sit down—she wasn't quite sure why—as she fumbled in her bag for her car keys. 'But I'm quite mobile really so you don't need to——'

'Fuss?' Wendy supplied with a twinkle. 'I won't. But I will do this. Be back in a tick.'

A charming . . . child, Juanita thought as she stared at the closed door, and, So you don't like elegant women, Mr Walker? What does that mean, I wonder?

She stood up and limped over to the window with a faint frown creasing her brow—and discovered her guest bedroom had a lovely view of the rolling scenery that made up the Bowral-Mittagong area of New South Wales, south of Sydney, now clothed in its summer gold and heady with the perfume of ripe grass seed. There were horses in well-fenced paddocks beyond a rather wild but wonderful garden that had sweeping lawns, shrubs and stands of gum spreading cool shade.

The house was built of mellow, quarried stone and was large, low, sprawling and creeper-hung. It had a steep slate roof, chimneys and some wonderful bow windows and, for its age, was in quite good condition but—she fingered the faded curtains and looked down at the threadbare carpet—was desperately in need of a refit. And despite the traumas of the morning and Gareth Walker's unsettling, to say the least, effect on her, she felt a quickening of interest as she looked around. It was her kind of house after all; it suited her particular talent, her love of antiques, her ability to blend the practicality of modern conveniences with the grace of bygone eras.

And, of course, there was more than the challenge of not only doing it and doing it to the satisfaction of its owner—she grimaced slightly—but the challenge after the time of pain and isolation, the years of always being the odd one out, the plain one, the untalented one, of proving herself to her family...

'This is Steven and this is Rebecca,' Gareth Walker said. 'This is Miss Spencer-Hill, kids—what did you say your first name was? Something unusual.' He regarded Juanita with a frown.

She told him and said, 'How do you do, Steven and Rebecca?' to the two children sitting at a vast table in the kitchen. The same two children who had been pummelling the life out of each other earlier and were, she saw with an inward smile, now looking chastened and scrubbed. They were also twins with fair hair and freckles and bore an undoubted resemblance to Wendy.

'Hello,' they said in unison.

'Never heard that name before,' Rebecca added. 'Why do you use a stick?'

'None of your business, Rebecca,' Wendy warned, coming to the table with a plate of cold meat. 'You've been bad enough as it is this morning without being nosey on top of it——'

'I just asked,' Rebecca broke in heatedly.

'That's true,' Gareth drawled, pulling out a chair for Juanita. 'Do sit down. I hope you don't mind us eating in the kitchen.' He turned back to Rebecca. 'Juanita is a Spanish name and, consistent with Spanish pronunciation, although it's spelt J.U.A.N.I.T.A, the J is said more like an H and the U and A are run together like this.' He said the name slowly. 'Got it?'

Both fair heads nodded.

'Good. The reason for the stick is because Juanita has a sore hip.'

'Why?' This was Steven.

'Because she has—end of subject. Eat your lunch,' he said coolly. 'Kids who talk too much and ask *too* many questions have been known to miss out on certain things.'

Both Steven and Rebecca turned their attention hastily to their plates.

It was a pleasant lunch of cold meat and salad followed by fruit and cheese, and during it Juanita learnt that Wendy's and the twins' mother had some complicated, non-fatal condition that nevertheless required corrective surgery and two months' recuperation; that their father had been killed in an accident not long after the twins were born and how Gareth had taken on the husbandless Mrs Spicer and her children soon afterwards; how they lived in an annexe attached to the house and, thus, how Wendy came to be filling in for her mother; how the twins had ended up being everyone's responsibility during this trying period and how, although they were beyond the spotty stage, they were recovering from chicken pox and therefore off school.

'So now you're "in the picture", Juanita,' Gareth said somewhat wryly from the head of the table.

'I am indeed,' she murmured, and sipped her tea. The twins had been dismissed and Wendy was working at the sink, humming a happy little tune.

He lay back in his chair. 'Think you can work in *these* conditions?' he queried, with an ironic little glint in his eyes.

Juanita frowned faintly, the irony not lost on her, but she said nothing.

'I thought,' he continued after waiting a moment, 'you might be reassured that this isn't some Bluebeard's Castle.'

Their eyes met across the table but Juanita had taken herself to task while she'd unpacked and prepared for lunch, and advised herself not to be drawn into any conversation that could re-create that astonishing lapse in her self-control. 'I never thought it was,' she said coolly. 'Er—how should we go about this, Mr Walker? Would you like to take me on a tour of the house and give me some idea of your preferences or would you rather I wandered around on my own then presented you with some ideas? If you've been consumed by inspiration— I presume you mean literary inspiration—the latter might save you some time.'

'On the other hand,' he drawled, 'I do have some definite preferences, Miss Spencer-Hill, so I think we should do it together otherwise the latter might only be a *waste* of time.'

Juanita tilted her head in a non-committal sort of way, as if to say, Have it your way, it's your money—which only had the effect of drawing a lightning grin from him as he stood up and walked round to hold her chair for her as she rose herself, and to hand her her stick. But in the moment that they stood close together she was struck again by the fact that this man affected her whether she liked it or not—and that he knew it. Wasn't that cool amusement she saw in his eyes as their gazes locked for an instant? She was quite sure it was as she felt herself colouring foolishly and felt, at the same time, a curious prickle of fear run down her spine.

Damn you, Gareth Walker, she thought, although she said evenly, 'Perhaps you'd like to lead the way?'

CHAPTER TWO

'THIS is the master bedroom.'

'What a wonderful room!' The words came out before Juanita could stop them and she had to flinch as she intercepted the quizzical look Gareth Walker cast her. 'Well, it is,' she added stubbornly, 'and I don't know why you should be looking at me like that, Mr Walker. Rooms are my business whatever they are.'

'Quite,' he agreed gravely. 'It just surprised me that the one room that really seems to have caught your imagination is a bedroom.'

Juanita grimaced. During their tour of the house thus far, she had been restrained, but because restrained was the way she'd decided to be, not because it hadn't all appealed to her. So to get caught out over a bedroom was somewhat galling—although why? she asked herself angrily. It was a beautifully proportioned room with a window-seat, with its own fireplace, a solarium attached, and, for all its faded furbishing, threadbare carpet and time-washed colours, it somehow represented the heart of the house.

'Not for any deep, dark reasons, I can assure you,' she heard herself say with scorn. 'Are you imagining I suffer from subliminal inclinations towards bedrooms? Really, Mr Walker——' she smiled at him coolly '—it's your mind that seems to stray in that direction constantly.'

'I would disagree with you there, Juanita,' he said mildly, 'but let's not argue. And since you seem to be so taken with this room, I think I might give you *carte*

blanche with it. How does that affect you?' He raised
an eyebrow at her.

Juanita looked at him narrowly. 'Why?'

'Why not?' he countered.

'Well...' she paused and glanced down at the clipboard in her hand upon which she'd been making notes
as they'd progressed through the house '...you do have
some definite preferences as you mentioned, so——' She
broke off and shrugged.

'And from the odd things you've let fall, you didn't
disagree with them.'

'I don't,' she said, looking up at last. 'On the other
hand my idea of a master bedroom might be quite different from yours. So I think you should at least tell me
whether you want it to be a very feminine kind of
room...' She paused. 'Ideally, of course, the lady of the
house should help design this room.'

'That would be true of the whole place but there is
no lady of the house.'

'A problem,' she conceded. 'Who was the last lady to
use it?'

'My wife.'

She couldn't help the little flare of shock that came
to her eyes. 'I didn't know you were married...'

'Why should you?'

'N-no reason. Um...so...?'

He smiled, but not with humour. 'For your infor-
mation, Miss Spencer-Hill, like you she was involved in
a car accident. Unlike you it proved to be fatal. It was
also quite a few years ago.'

'I'm sorry,' Juanita said awkwardly and feeling as if
she'd been unforgivably intrusive.

'All the furnishings and so on in this house date much
further back than that, though. She didn't have the time

to make her mark on it, you could say. So you won't be eradicating anything of hers.'

'I see. Well...' She hesitated.

'What now?' he said coolly.

Juanita frowned and couldn't help inwardly trying to assess what kind of emotion lay behind this apparently emotionless résumé of Gareth Walker's loss. Not that I'd expect him to bare his soul, but why do I detect a sound of discord? she thought.

'Look,' he said then, 'I detest frills and furbelows, satin and lace, dolls and silk sheets—does that help?'

'Yes,' she said baldly.

He raised a quizzical eyebrow at her. 'You say that as if I were accusing you of liking those things. I wasn't. I—would hope your taste is much more subtle and elegant.'

'It is,' she said tartly before she could stop herself, but that word elegant did it. 'Although I do find certain irregularities in what you say and what you really regard as elegant—such as women who look as if they've stepped out of a magazine.' She stopped abruptly and wished she'd held her peace.

His eyes rested on her face expressionlessly for a moment then he frowned faintly. 'That rings a bell. Why it should concern you, though, escapes me as well. Do enlighten me, Juanita.'

She bit her lip but there was *no* escaping his steady, speculative gaze. 'You told me I was elegant earlier. You apparently told Wendy once that you detested——'

'Ah! I remember. As a rule I do detest those kind of women but I also said that to Wendy when she was going through a stage of trying to look like a thirty-year-old vamp. And yours, Miss Spencer-Hill, is a different kind of elegance, so you may unruffle your feathers,' he finished softly.

'How——?' Juanita broke off and could have bitten her tongue. What is *wrong* with me? she wondered. 'It doesn't matter,' she said stiffly and moved away to sit down on the end of the bed, laying her stick beside her.

He studied her for a moment then pulled one of the chairs set before the fireplace round and sat down opposite her. 'I'll tell you.' He rested his elbows on the arms of the chair and formed his fingers into a steeple beneath his chin. 'Elegance is a state of mind, I think. It does not follow fashion slavishly and however ridiculous it may be, nor does it always need to be excessively groomed and painted. Does that answer your question?'

Juanita blinked. 'But you would have to know someone better than you know me to—know whether I have it—the state of mind, I mean as opposed to looking as if one has stepped out of a magazine.'

'As a writer, one tends to be a student of human nature—I know,' he said simply.

'Then you must know me better than I know myself,' she retorted sharply.

'It's possible,' he commented.

'No, it's not! We've only just met!'

'All the same I'd be amazed if I were wrong. What upsets you so much about it?'

Juanita stood up and limped over to the bay window. 'It's too—*personal*,' she said intensely.

'You brought it up,' he pointed out with considerable irony.

'No, you brought it all up in the first place,' she said raggedly. 'When I'd been here barely five minutes and then you set out to make me uncomfortable over a bedroom——'

'My dear,' he drawled, 'your sensitivity amazes me and I have to wonder what's behind it. Could it be that you're secretly longing for some strange man to pin you to some strange bed? You know, we all have our fantasies, there's nothing so dreadful in it, but——'

'If *anyone* is suffering from bizarre fantasies it's much more likely to be you,' she shot at him.

'Assuming I was suffering from any kind of fantasies regarding you, Miss Spencer-Hill,' he said drily, 'I get the feeling they're not entirely unreciprocated.'

She swung round from the window, her eyes dark and suddenly confused. 'I h-haven't done a thing to let you th-think that!' she protested, but stammering and confused by the dry, not at all insolent but curiously thoughtful way he'd said what he had and his different expression, as well as being attacked by guilt as she remembered how she'd been stopped in her tracks earlier by his proximity.

He smiled, but differently again. And said reflectively but with pitiless mockery all the same, 'Yes. It really wouldn't be impossible for our fantasies to coincide, you know, despite the extreme brevity of our acquaintance. Human nature is a strange thing, and the chemistry between the sexes is often stranger. Wouldn't you agree?' he finished simply and raised a wry eyebrow at her.

'*Agree* . . . ?' Juanita stared at him and could get no further words out as, to her horror, her gaze was pulled inexorably towards the bed.

'Of course,' he went on idly, 'we would have to be sure that it was genuine spontaneous chemistry and not, for example, a subtle or not so subtle campaign for you to end up in my bed—for other reasons.'

'Wh-what?' she whispered, going red and pale by turns. 'You must be joking!'

'Not at all,' he said gravely. 'I have enough money and fame to . . .' he paused ' . . . be imposed upon by members of the opposite sex from time to time.'

She gasped. 'Do you—are you accusing me of disguising myself as an interior decorator? Do you think——?'

'No.' He looked amused. 'I was merely making it known to you that, while you appear to be paranoid about—being imposed upon by men you've barely met, I have the same problem with some women——'

But he got no further because Juanita flung her clipboard at him. It missed its mark and he picked it up off the floor beside him and smoothed the pages before looking up at her. 'So you have a temper too. Go on,' he said ruefully. 'I foresee some interesting times ahead.'

'I think you're destestable, Mr Walker,' she ground out. 'I am *not* one of those women and despite your wishful thinking I have had no fantasies concerning you at all!'

'Good,' he said mildly. 'Shall we continue our tour?'

She stared at him, her breasts heaving, her mouth working, then she picked up her stick and walked out ahead of him.

'So—that's the full extent of it. Tired?'

Juanita shook her head, her eyes still stormy, which caused him merely to smile faintly. All the same she was grateful to sit down in his study if for no other reason than to gather her wits and mentally castigate herself for losing her cool to the incredible extent of throwing things...and indulging in unbelievable mental images...

'What do you think?'

She glanced down at the notes she'd made and said with an effort, 'It's a big project.'

'It should have been done years ago—as you can see. But the structure is sound and in good repair.'

'Yes.'

'You don't think you can do it?' he queried with a tinge of impatience after waiting a moment. 'Or *isn't* it to your taste, the way I want it?'

Juanita chewed her lip. In broad outline his concept of what he wanted had so far met with her approval entirely. So had his desire to keep as many of the old pieces of furniture as possible, although he'd said he didn't want to re-create the original period that the house had been furnished and decorated in—'In other words I don't want it looking like a museum,' had been his exact words. 'Yes, it is,' she said reluctantly.

'What's the problem, then?' He was definitely impatient now, his blue eyes narrowed and probing.

'There is more to decorating a house than just choosing colour schemes et cetera,' she said slowly. 'I like to spend quite a bit of time studying things like—the light factor in each room, the ambience of rooms—is this one a busy, cheerful room or a peaceful one?—and so on. I like—it's hard to explain—but I like to get the feel of a house and the people who live in it.'

'You have *carte blanche* to do all that—I told you.'

'And I told you,' she said evenly, 'that I would take the minimum amount of time possible. I have to confess that I spoke in the heat of the moment and I may have misled you—it would take at the very least a month to complete a job like this, and that would probably be rushing it. Not, of course, that I would spend all that time staying here but I'd have to be in and out quite a lot—and one can't just pop in and out down here.'

'So what you're telling me in fact is that you don't care to spend that amount of time on my house?'

Juanita took a careful breath. 'I'm saying,' she said quietly, 'that we might have problems working in such proximity——'

'Here we go again—for someone whose career could suffer if you lose this job one would almost think you were out to self-destruct, Miss Spencer-Hill,' he drawled. 'Why should it be a problem? Because I *do* disturb you in some way and the thought of—getting the "feel" of me——' his lips quirked '—and my house disturbs you all the more?'

'Because I think you're going out of your way to upset me,' she retorted, stung.

'How?'

She coloured angrily. 'I don't *believe* you—but take what you just said for example—you managed to turn an ordinary phrase into something...s-something...else!'

He laughed outright. 'My apologies—I couldn't resist it. All right, perhaps we got off on the wrong foot earlier,' he said, his former impatience returning, 'and lapsed lamentably——' his eyes glinted a deep, ironic blue '—into the games men and women play, although I still deny I was motivated by anything other than the fact that you're unusually striking—and vulnerable, a curious combination—but there was no more to it than that. How could there be? Although...' he paused '...your super-sensitivity on the subject seemed to—fuel things along.' He looked thoughtful. 'Should we examine another scenario in our bid to clarify things between us, Miss Spencer-Hill? Do you nurture a deep, dark hatred of men? Do——?'

'*No.*'

'Just—no?' he queried.

'Just no,' she agreed stiffly, clamping down on the hot words that she would have liked to say instead.

'Well, then——' he surveyed her meditatively, not at all put out by the scathing look she just couldn't help that he received in return '—is it on or off? I must tell you I had no idea I would have to go through all this in order to bestow an inordinate amount of money, no doubt, on a firm of interior decorators.'

'And I must tell you——' she just couldn't help herself any longer '—that I despise the way you fall into the *games* men and women play——'

He swore then. 'What are you?' he demanded. 'A nun in disguise?'

'Of course not. Just someone who isn't prepared to lay herself open for weeks to that k-kind of thing.' Even as she said it, she knew it sounded pompous and a little ridiculous and she found herself dearly wishing, too late, that she'd never allowed this conversation to develop.

'If you imagine I intend to play games with you for weeks, Miss Spencer-Hill, you're wrong,' he said coldly. 'Will you do it or won't you?'

She hesitated. He hadn't sat down himself but was leaning his broad shoulders against a bookcase. Two walls of the room, in fact, were lined with books, there was a word processor on a second desk, there were stacks of papers and more books on most available surfaces and where there weren't bookshelves on the wall there were paintings of horses and one exquisite landscape framed in gold against the dark green wallpaper. And there was a rug on the floor that glowed with greens and golds and muted ruby. It was an untidy room but, unlike the rest of the house, she realised suddenly, it had obviously recently been decorated, and as her gaze roamed around she knew she wouldn't change any of it, so if he'd done it himself they did have very similar tastes ...

'Did you do this room?' she asked involuntarily.

'Yes.' He raised an eyebrow. 'Any objections?'

She shook her head a bit confusedly. Am I being a fool? she wondered, and, Why *am* I being like this? Because of a few bitter little experiences whereby I've been made aware some men imagine that when you limp and stammer, when you're flawed, in other words, you're grateful for any crumbs they might throw your way... But has this been quite the same kind of thing? Have I *fuelled* things along, so to speak? But how can he sense the effect he had on me and what right does it give him to...to...? Anyway, now I'm aware of the pitfalls, surely I can reverse things...

'I'll do it,' she said abruptly. 'But there is something else.'

'I'm waiting,' he murmured with a grimace.

'Do you live here completely alone?'

His eyes narrowed. 'Why do you ask?'

'Well, it just doesn't have a lived-in aura, the house.' She paused. 'That's not quite true, there is a *bygone* aura but—well, I'm asking because it's hard to get the f——' She stopped, then continued, 'It's hard to know——' She broke off again, frustratedly, then said baldly, 'Without a woman in residence, it's—a little hard, that's all. I did mention that earlier.'

He studied her enigmatically. 'So you did, in relation to the master bedroom.' He paused as her gaze flickered. 'Perhaps you'd care to explain further?'

Juanita took a steadying breath and thought for a moment. 'Women generally have a feeling for their houses, and not only their bedrooms—a more practical feeling——' she glanced at him and dared him to laugh, which he didn't '—because they usually spend more time in them and they're the ones who have to make them work or put up with their shortcomings. And it means more to them, I think, if they loath a particular colour or whatever.'

'I see. So what you're saying is your efforts could be a waste of time should I take a wife who detests it all— I have no plans in that direction,' he said gravely. 'And

I can't allow the place to fall to pieces in the interim, can I?'

'No. No.' She bit her lip.

'What now?'

'I wasn't trying t-to——'

'Pry?'

'No, I wasn't,' she said evenly. 'Perhaps it's because I've never worked with a man before, not on a house at least,' she amended, 'that I feel a little at sea.'

'You're a woman,' he pointed out politely.

'I do know that,' she responded tartly.

'Earlier you didn't seem to think it was of any importance.'

'It's not—I'm not the woman who is going to have to live here——'

'Heaven help her,' he said softly.

Juanita blushed. 'I didn't say that!'

'You looked it.' He moved at last and sat down facing her on the edge of the walnut desk and the way he looked at her was with serious attention which she just knew was a mockery.

She gritted her teeth. 'Don't start again, Mr Walker.'

His eyes glinted wickedly but he said obligingly, 'All right. I don't know what it is about you that brings out these impulses in me; I shall have to try to curb them— believe it or not I rather appreciate the way *you've* taken in the aura of this house. So yes, it is unlived-in mostly at present. I spend a lot of time overseas researching my books, and the rest of the family—I have six brothers and sisters—have all gone their own way, although they do tend to descend from time to time; but it's lacked a woman in charge, other than a housekeeper, for quite a few years and, as I have no plans to remarry, is likely to remain so. But it was a happy, comfortable place in its time and if you can pick up those vibes as well as adding any—practical feminine touches of your own, I think—well, I think it's the best that can be done, don't you?'

Surprise caused her dark eyes to widen. It had sounded so reasonable. 'Y-yes.' She hesitated then shrugged. 'All right. Well, I might do a bit of work now. You'll probably be wanting to get to work yourself.'

He looked faintly wry then said curiously, 'What will you be doing?'

'Some sketches, taking some photos and measurements. I don't suppose you have the original plans?'

'As a matter of fact I do.'

'Oh!' Her eyes lit up. 'That's wonderful. I also have some samples in the car that you might like to take a look at—material swatches, that is—but we can leave that until later,' she said hastily, whereupon he smiled outright.

'Don't worry so. I fully intend to leave you to it. Do you know,' he added, 'you looked like a different person a moment ago—before you clamped down on your enthusiasm? Alive and quite beautiful.'

Juanita looked down at her hands, confused and disturbed by him once again. And hoping against hope that he didn't really know that he disturbed her in the way he did.

'How long ago was this accident, Juanita?' he said suddenly into the silence.

She looked up. 'Three years ago.'

'That's a fair while.'

She grimaced. 'I know, but broken bones and other things can take a long time to heal and I—broke quite a few. I couldn't walk for a time but I'm fine now.'

'And before the accident?'

'What do you mean?'

'What was your life like?'

She lowered her lashes. 'Much the same as anyone's, probably.'

'Did you always have an ambition to be an interior decorator?'

'I...' She paused. 'No. I wasn't quite sure what I wanted to be or that there was anything I would be good at.'

'That——' he narrowed his eyes '—seems to represent a certain lack of confidence.'

'Does it? A lot of people don't know what they want to do——'

'The fact that you didn't think there was anything you would be good at part.'

Juanita considered and hoped he wouldn't guess how right he was. Then she grimaced. 'You're right. My stammer accounted for some of it and...' she hesitated '...other things.'

'Such as?'

She sighed. 'I've no idea why you find this so fascinating but perhaps if we get it out of the way for once and for all we could both do some work. I think I was born one of those shy, ill-at-ease people. I was certainly the only untalented one in the family, inarticulate, thin, gawky—I wouldn't have blamed my mother for wondering whether there'd been a mix-up of babies at birth; I don't even look much like them. And I was a shy, awkward teenager, and later. Then things happened the way they did and I had that to get over as well. If you're wondering whether any of it accounts for—a certain prickliness I've shown, it probably does but, curiously, being confined to a wheelchair for a time made me realise how lucky I'd been before and gave me the determination not to allow myself to spend the rest of my life in a sea of self-consciousness, and to make something of it.'

'I see. *Bravo* again,' he murmured. 'How come you got this job? I mean, Bluemoon is a very—*in* firm of interior decorators. All the best people use them, so I'm told.' He looked amused.

'I'd finished a Bachelor of Arts before the accident and I did an interior decorating course mainly by correspondence while I was recuperating—almost by accident. I mean, I virtually chose something to do at random although I had always loved furniture and wood and so on, and it wasn't long before I was enthralled. So I took the first job I could get when I was able to, which was with Bluemoon—well, I've worked my way up since.'

'You must have considerable flair, though,' he said musingly. 'Twenty-five doesn't seem very old to be let loose like this.'

Juanita smiled faintly. 'It's my first major job. I'm...pretty much on trial.'

'You could have fooled me!'

Juanita looked rueful. 'Well, now you know. I've gone from being tongue-tied to shrewish. Would you mind very much if I got to work?'

But he frowned faintly. 'Not exactly shrewish but very much on the defensive. Almost,' he reflected, 'as if there was something about *me* that had put you on your guard before you'd even met me.'

Juanita rose. 'You don't think it could have been anything to do with being greeted the way I was?' she asked ironically.

He moved a long, strong hand idly and his eyes glinted quizzically. 'I think it was more than that.'

Juanita bit her lip then tried to say airily, 'No. W-what time is d-dinner?'

'The dead give-away,' he commented. 'I mean, when you start stammering—what have I done to make you nervous now?'

'N-not a thing,' she said, moving to the door but foolishly feeling a dew of sweat break out on the back of her neck. What *is* wrong with me? she thought.

He caught her at the door and put his hand on the handle before she could. 'It has to be something—I thought we'd sorted out all our problems?'

'We have,' she said, her voice quivering with effort.

'Tell me another,' he replied brusquely. 'Is there some good reason why you should have taken an instantaneous dislike to me, Juanita? Something you've heard about me or read about me—I can assure you nine-tenths of what other people write about people like me is imagination.'

'No,' she denied. 'I mean, the only thing I know about you is from what I saw on television once so—er—I haven't even r-read one of your books.'

'How damning,' he marvelled. 'You should, you know, they're good.'

'How modest,' she marvelled. 'They may be but I don't think they're my kind of reading.'

'How do you know until you've tried one?'

Juanita drew a breath. 'All right, I will,' she said exasperatedly. 'I thought you said you were going to let me get on with it?'

'That was until you got all bitter and twisted again,' he drawled.

'I'm *not*!' she cried.

The sudden silence was deafening. Juanita stared at him, stunned by the emotion of her reaction. Nor did he break the silence immediately but he took his time examining the way her eyes were dilated and the way she was breathing—he did that by quite pointedly dropping his gaze to her breasts, which were rising and falling agitatedly beneath the Liberty print.

'Oh,' she whispered and went to turn away abruptly but he caught her wrist and held it in his long fingers in a grip that was impossible to break.

'I'm not letting you go, Juanita,' he warned, 'until I find out why you're in such a state.'

'I'm not . . . you have no right . . . it's because you're *impossible* and you're still being unbelievably personal—talk about prying,' she said disjointedly, trying to gather some control. 'You have to be the end!'

He merely looked wry. 'I told you just now that because I'm a writer I'm also a student of human nature. Well, that's part of it. But perhaps there is more at work here than meets the eye,' he said thoughtfully, and relaxed his grip on her wrist but didn't release it. 'Haven't there been *any* men in your life, Juanita?'

'That's *my* business,' she flashed. 'Look! How would you have reacted if I'd barged in here and asked you why you have no plans to get married again or . . . or . . .' she stopped and groped for something else appropriate to fling at him—and even surprised herself a bit with what she came up with '. . . demanded to know what gives you the right to reduce television interviewers to simpering, dithering idiots and think you can do it to me? Don't *laugh*!' she finished through her teeth.

'I can't help it,' he said, but sobered. 'So that's it— I didn't set out to reduce her to a *simpering* idiot.'

'Heaven help the woman you set out to do that to. What about dithering, then; do you admit to that?'

'My dear, there were certain cross-currents at work that you may not have been aware of. I had been told that Laura Hennessey regarded my books as lightweight and that she didn't believe they deserved the popularity

they enjoyed. Much the same as your sentiments probably——'

'Who told you that?'

He grimaced. 'Her secretary, who made all the
arrangements.'

'How come?'

He looked wry.

'I can imagine,' Juanita said sardonically. 'You took
the time to chat her up, no doubt.'

'Very nicely, though,' he conceded.

'If you think that makes it any better!'

'I do.' He eyed her ingenuously.

Juanita made a disgusted sound. 'So then you set out
to slay Laura——'

'No,' he said in a different tone. 'I set out to defend
my right to write what I like and to defend the people
who enjoy reading my books, who number in their millions, incidentally. She found she couldn't come up with
anything to say other than that they weren't exactly literature with a capital L, which is what a lot of people
use to define literature that doesn't sell well, as I pointed
out to her. Now why she should have found that so difficult to cope with, an interviewer of her stature, is not
something you can hold me responsible for.'

'No?' Juanita said slowly as her mind ranged back to
the interview and some further scales could be said to
fall from her mind's eye. 'There's got to be a lesson learnt
from that . . .' she murmured.

'There has?'

Juanita closed her eyes in frustration because she'd
spoken her thoughts aloud. When she opened them it
was to stare directly into the dark blue depths of his,
and suddenly become aware that he was running one
finger gently up and down the inside of her wrist.

'You were saying?' he murmured.

Never to underestimate the power of your sheer mas-
culine appeal and I don't believe that you're unaware of
it or that you don't use it deliberately and in a quite
unprincipled way... I think that's what I was saying
although I won't be saying it to you, the thought ran
through her mind. So what do I do about the fact that
I'm virtually pinned here unable to remove myself from
your grasp—unable or unwilling?

'It doesn't matter. Would you mind letting me go?'

He lifted her wrist and inspected it briefly then re-
stored her hand to her side. 'I hope there are no bruises.
You should have told me you were such a Laura
Hennessey fan and such a feminist, after all.'

'I'm not——' Juanita bit her lip. 'I mean, no more
than normal. And how you fight your battles has nothing
to do with me.' She shrugged.

He smiled. 'Other than to lower myself in your esti-
mation even more?'

She said nothing.

He raised an eyebrow, but said merely. 'Well, off you
go. Please do make use of all our facilities. There's a
swimming-pool round the back, horses to ride, and so
on.'

'Thank you, I don't ride, though.'

'Do you swim?'

'Er—yes.'

'Good. Dinner, by the way, is at seven.'

CHAPTER THREE

THANKS to Wendy, Juanita was made uncomfortably aware that she would be dining alone with Gareth Walker.

'Oh, please,' she said after she'd finished work and Wendy had come along to her bedroom to check that she had everything she needed and impart the news, 'there's no need for that. Couldn't we all have it together as we had lunch?'

'Well, we do usually but I like to make an exception when Gareth has guests,' Wendy said seriously, then her pretty fresh face creased into a grin. 'I've never done it before,' she confided. 'I've been dying to have the opportunity while Mum's away to make a special meal and set the table in the dining-room—I asked Gareth and he said, "Why not?" I'm starting a catering course as soon as Mum gets back. Gareth is helping me pay for it, although I intend to pay him back, of course—I love cooking!'

It was impossible to protest further in the face of such shining enthusiasm. 'Thank you very much,' Juanita murmured. 'You're lucky to have—been in this position while your mother's in hospital.'

'Weren't we ever? We've been lucky since the first day we got here! Would you believe Rebecca and Steven getting chicken pox the day after Mum went to hospital, though? I don't know how I would have coped without Gareth.'

'He helped?' Juanita said, unwittingly fascinated.

'He's *really* good with kids.' Wendy shook her pony-
tail as if to add emphasis to this. 'He read to them, did
jigsaw puzzles and so on, and no one can calm them
down the way Gareth can, not even Mum. It's such a
pity!'

Juanita lifted an eyebrow. 'What is?'

'That he lost his own child. And his wife too, of
course. They were killed in an accident. It was all before
we came here. The child was only a baby, a little boy.
Oh, look, I'd better dash or my dinner won't be worth
eating. Will you—change?'

Juanita stared at her, then smiled belatedly.
'Certainly!'

Wendy beamed back and scampered off.

What into, though? Juanita asked herself some time later
after a shower, staring at her limited wardrobe, which
hadn't been put together with festive dinners in mind.

In the end she chose a serviceable fawn skirt and a
silky, sleeveless cream blouse which she wore with a brilliant amber scarf around her hips. It still didn't look as
dressy as she suspected Wendy had in mind, but would
have to do, she decided.

Then she opened her bedroom door a crack and heard
Steven saying importantly, 'Can I light the candles, Wen?
I've put the wine in the silver cooler.'

She closed the door with a grimace and went to stare
at her image in the mirror, and reflect that she didn't
look much different from how she looked going to work.
So she reached for her jewel-case which she always travelled with and took out her grandmother's pearls. She'd
inherited them on her twenty-first birthday and wore
them a lot, as one should with pearls, but often beneath
her clothes. She put them on over her blouse and chose
a wide gold bracelet to wear as well.

But the effect, although improved, was still rather severe and with a sudden movement she released her hair, which she'd tied back as normal. Her hair was what she thought of as her one asset. It was almost black, strong and full of body and with the sheen of rough silk, and it was all one length to just above her shoulders. The difference was quite startling. Her features seemed to acquire a new delicacy, her eyes looked larger and her skin, very lightly made-up, in contrast to the mass of dark, buoyant hair, seemed no longer slightly sallow but arrestingly smooth, clear and pale.

She lifted a wry eyebrow and wondered if she was imagining things then her eyes fell on the little vase of camellia blooms Wendy had put on the dressing-table; with a shrug akin to feeling that she might as well be hung for a sheep as a lamb, she pulled one out, dried the stem carefully with tissues, pruned it a bit with her nail scissors, and pinned it into her hair.

'Wow!' Rebecca said as Juanita walked into the dining-room where they all appeared to be assembled.

'You look stunning!' Steven said in awe-struck tones.

'You do too!' Wendy bustled forward and took her hand. 'Do you like it?' She drew her towards the smaller of the two tables that inhabited the huge dining-room. This one was set in the bow window, and set for two with gleaming silver and crystal, starched pink damask and an intricate and rather lovely centre-piece of more camellia blooms and their dark green leaves. There were also two plates of salad, artistically arranged, already set.

Juanita's eyes softened as she studied the table and she said, after inspecting it all carefully, 'It would do credit to a really top restaurant, Wendy. It's lovely.'

Wendy positively glowed, then she became businesslike. 'Everything's ready on the sideboard, keeping hot so you can serve yourselves. I thought that would be better than me popping in and out all the time but if you do need anything just give me a yell! Come along, kids.'

'But ... Can't ... ?'

'Come *along*, kids.'

They went, not without some good-natured grumbling, and for the first time Juanita looked fully at Gareth Walker, who had stood a little apart and said nothing so far.

He too had changed—into a pair of dark trousers, a long-sleeved white shirt and a blue tie. His thick hair was damp and brushed, and he looked tall, sophisticated—and amused as his gaze lingered on her loose hair and the flower in it.

'Don't imagine,' Juanita said drily, and bit her lip.

'I won't. What did you think I would imagine, though?' He lifted an eyebrow at her.

'What I meant to say,' Juanita said carefully, 'was that this is—a mock-up if you like, because I didn't bring anything very dressy, and it's all for Wendy's benefit.'

'Of course,' he murmured. 'Just the same you—"mock-up" rather sensationally.' He strolled forward at last and pulled out one of the chairs. 'Would you care to be seated, Miss Spencer-Hill?'

'Th-thank you,' she said stiffly, doing just that and occupying herself with her napkin as he withdrew the wine from its frosted silver cooler and uncorked it.

'Perhaps this will help.' He poured some golden liquid into her glass.

'Help?'

He didn't reply immediately but poured his own then sat down. 'Help to—ease us into the kind of pleasant, amiable meal that will come up to Wendy's expectations.'

Juanita said nothing. But she did take a sip of her wine and she did raise her glass in a slight acknowledgement of his observation.

But it was halfway through the salad that they spoke at all and it was she who rather ruefully broke the impasse. 'I seem to have told you an awful lot about myself. Would you consider returning the compliment?'

He looked up enigmatically. 'What would you like to know?'

She considered. 'How you came to be a writer.'

He put his fork down and shrugged. 'Like you,' he said slowly, 'there was a time when I didn't know what I wanted to be, although it was more a matter of making a choice. I had two great attractions—journalism and politics. No, make that three—a real sense of wanderlust as well. So I studied both journalism and political science and when I graduated I was lucky enough to get on to the foreign desk of a major paper and thus—bring it all together.' He grimaced. 'So for a number of years I roamed the world in search of stories and covered momentous events, political and otherwise.'

'That's it?' Juanita queried after a longish pause during which they both finished their starter.

'More or less. Well, along the way I inherited this place, which was rather run-down and becoming a liability. My father used to breed, school and agist polo ponies but that operation too had run down and suffered a lot of mismanagement in his declining years; it had got to the stage of actually costing money and I had the alternative of selling up entirely or trying to get it going again. That and other circumstances persuaded me to come home eventually and settle down. Which was not as easy as it sounded,' he said.

'No, I can believe that,' Juanita remarked slowly. 'And that's when you decided to put all your experiences to use and write the kind of political thrillers you do?'

'That's it in a nutshell, ma'am!' His lips twisted. 'So I wrote like the devil and in between times I schooled polo ponies and gradually built up that side of things, and as I began to be successful as a writer I began to restore the house structurally—a new roof, I had it re-wired, rebuilt some chimneys, new hot-water systems and so on. I was just about to embark on the bathrooms as a matter of fact when it occurred to me a decorator might be more—handy.'

Why she said it she wasn't sure but she did. 'It sounds—rather lonely.' She wrinkled her brow.

He looked at her a shade cynically, she thought. But he said gravely, 'Not at all. My youngest sister Xanthe, who is just twenty-two now, managed to—er—enliven my life considerably, not to mention age me at the same time. But of course once the dollars started flowing in and Xanthe left home, I was able to indulge my other passion—travelling—and combine it with gathering new material for books. Would you like to embark on the second course? It smells delicious.'

'Thank you, but can I——?'

'Not at all. You're the guest.'

Juanita stayed seated and sipped some more wine while he dished up what turned out to be lemon chicken and rice, and was delicious.

'Mmm. I think Wendy is on the right track,' she murmured after a couple of mouthfuls.

'I hope so. She's a nice kid.'

'You've obviously been very good to them,' Juanita commented.

'It hasn't been hard.'

They ate in silence until he refilled their glasses and said, 'Have we run out of pleasant, amiable conversation?'

Juanita looked at him a little narrowly through her lashes. 'I introduced the last topic.'

'So you did.' He pushed his plate away and sat back, idly running his fingers around the base of his glass. 'Well, then—what keeps you from being lonely, Juanita?'

She looked at him more fully and detected—there was no doubt about it this time—that glint of cynicism in his eyes again. She hesitated briefly before saying evenly, 'I wasn't being gratuitously curious——'

'Does that mean you weren't wondering about my love-life?' His lips twisted wryly.

'No. Not exactly...' She paused and some confusion showed in her eyes. 'I merely expressed what came to mind, that's all,' she finished with a grimace. 'Why do men always assume one shares their eternal curiosity about people's love-lives?'

'Do they?'

'It's certainly a topic they find hard to stay away from,' she said tartly.

He looked at her amusedly. 'Someone said—I've never known who but I once read the observation that men come to love through sex and women come to sex through love. Do you think that accounts for it—assuming it's true?'

Juanita stared at him, curiously arrested. 'Do you mean that men have to sleep with someone before they can fall in love—or that sex is more important to them than anything else?'

He smiled faintly. 'I didn't make the original deduction. I was simply offering it as a theory. But most people would, I think, concede that sex plays a major part in any loving relationship.'

'And a major role in what may not be a loving relationship, necessarily, for men,' she said slowly. 'It certainly implies men seem to need to do a lot of experimenting. I wonder if it was a man or a woman who said that?'

He didn't reply. Instead he watched her enigmatically until she began to feel uncomfortable and then said rashly, 'Why are you looking at me like that?'

He shrugged. 'How?'

'As if you know *all* the answers while I'm fumbling around like a retarded . . . schoolgirl.'

'Have you ever been in love?'

'That's——'

'None of my business,' he said with soft mockery.

'All right! No, I haven't,' she retorted defiantly. 'Which doesn't mean to say I haven't had the usual kind of crushes but they've all come and gone without leaving me devastated.'

'And that's what you base your assumption that they couldn't have been love on?' he queried.

'Wouldn't you?'

He moved his shoulders and looked at her thoughtfully. 'I don't know. Have you allowed yourself to get really close to anyone?'

Juanita blinked. 'N-not . . . that close, no.'

'A real loner,' he commented. 'And thus—a virgin, no doubt.'

'No doubt,' she echoed sardonically although a tinge of colour came to her cheeks. 'You say that as if it's some sort of unpleasant disease,' she added coldly.

'Not at all. Just a crying shame,' he murmured, and his gaze lingered on her bare arms, the smooth curve of her throat, her hair. 'Well,' he said pleasantly then, 'should we try the dessert?'

But Juanita was suddenly fuming, she discovered. 'You can't simply say things like that and expect to get away with it!'

He looked at her quizzically. 'What did you have in mind?'

'I should very much like to slap your face,' she said through her teeth.

He grinned and his teeth were very white against his tan, his eyes devastatingly blue, and he looked big, totally relaxed and more than a match for her in every way.

'*Oh* . . . !' She flung her napkin down as if she was about to rise.

He sobered. 'In view of the pains you went to—purely for Wendy's benefit, of course—wouldn't it be a shame to spoil it all the same?' he drawled.

She sank back but said angrily, 'What are you implying now?'

He pushed his plate away. 'Let's be honest,' he said coolly. 'We're curious about each other. In that particular way men and women are.' There was no mistaking the significance of the way he was looking at her. 'But,' he continued, 'for reasons best known to yourself, it infuriates *you*, and for reasons all too well known to me I'm somewhat cynical about it all. None of that, however,' he said drily, 'can change that slight charge between us.' He raised his glass and drained it. 'I've said it before but I perceive interesting times ahead for us, Miss Spencer-Hill.'

Juanita opened her mouth, knew immediately she would stammer atrociously so she took a deep breath, waited for about ten seconds, then said protestingly, 'It's only been . . . it hasn't even been twenty-four hours!'

He smiled but it didn't reach his eyes. 'I wouldn't call you a retarded schoolgirl but you have to be astonishingly naïve.' He paused, watched her reflectively then murmured, 'Which would be another bar to anything coming to fruition between us, so—should we try to concentrate our energies on the dessert after all?'

As she went about her business the next day, Juanita was at pains to rid her mind of the frustrating conversation she'd foolishly allowed herself to indulge in the night before. Fortunately Wendy had intervened with coffee before they'd got the chance to concentrate on dessert, and Gareth had persuaded her to join them. Then he'd excused himself—and she hadn't laid eyes on him since.

She'd had an early night herself after helping Wendy with the dishes, and an early start today. The birdsong had woken her at the crack of dawn and she'd taken herself to the kitchen to make a cup of tea—and found, neatly bundled on the kitchen table, the plans of the house together with details of all the alterations.

Whether or not this had been a tacit indication that Gareth Walker did not intend to have speech with her on this wonderful clear summer morning she wasn't sure, but it certainly gave her something to get her teeth into, and she worked all morning on the four bathrooms which would constitute the major alterations she would be responsible for.

Wendy took the twins off for a visit to their mother about mid-morning, with instructions for what she'd left for lunch and saying she'd be back in time for dinner, which she'd already prepared and only needed heating up. But at midday, when there had still been no sign of Gareth Walker—he was holed up in his study, according to Wendy—Juanita balked at the idea of sharing another meal with him should he emerge, and she drove herself into Mittagong, where she had a snack and spent a couple of hours with the local tradesmen, checking out the viability of her ideas, showing them the plans and discussing the men's availability.

It was four o'clock when she got back, and her wonderful, clear summer morning had turned into a blindingly hot afternoon which made the sparkling blue waters of the pool look like an oasis in the desert.

She hesitated only briefly. There was no sight or sound of a living soul as she changed into her jade one-piece swimsuit, added a topaz filmy shirt, thanked her lucky stars that some whim had prompted her to include them in her luggage, and limped out to the pool.

The water was wonderful, and swimming the one physical exercise she could do well, and should do more of, she thought ruefully and guiltily. But of course there was a difference between swimming for pleasure on a hot, hot day and swimming because one should. In fact so great was the pleasure today, as she changed her strokes, swam underwater and generally frolicked, that she didn't notice she was not alone until at last she swam to the steps—and found Gareth Walker waiting there with a hand outstretched to help her out. Which caused her some confusion; she actually swallowed some water and finally came out coughing and spluttering.

'My apologies,' he said wryly, still holding her hand as she stood before him dripping. 'I didn't mean to frighten the life out of you.'

'I th-thought there was no one about,' she stammered.

He released her hand at last and handed her a towel. 'There wasn't. I've only this minute come up from the stables.'

Juanita breathed deeply and brushed her hair out of her eyes with her fingers. He wore a sky-blue T-shirt, khaki jodhpurs and long brown boots and he looked dusty and sweaty but vibrantly alive; it was impossible not to be disturbingly aware of his physique, of the broadness of his shoulders, the strong tanned throat, lean hips—and to picture how well he would look on a horse.

'I was—was just so h-hot,' she said, and wondered why she should keep sounding as if she was making excuses.

Something that was not lost on him, unfortunately. He said, 'No one in their right mind could resist the pool on a day like today—don't look so guilty. Why shouldn't you swim? Which you do like a mermaid, incidentally.'

'I thought you said you'd only this minute come——' She broke off and bit her lip.

He shrugged. 'A figure of speech, but I certainly wasn't here longer than three minutes at the most. Are you implying——' a wicked little glint lit his eyes as his gaze quite blatantly skimmed down her dripping costume that was moulded to her body and left not a lot of her figure to the imagination, including her taut nipples '—that qualifies me as a Peeping Tom?'

Am I? *Why* am I? she asked herself as she turned away without replying to hide the colour that had come to her cheeks. Because there is this charge—amend that, *slight* charge—between us whether I like it or not and to feel virtually naked in front of him is...rather devastating?

So devastating, she realised a moment later, as the sensation that had begun in her breasts, already sensitive from the cooler water, travelled down her body, that she had unwittingly begun to rub herself dry briskly in case he could guess or even see what was happening to her. The thought alone made her go hot and cold and she dropped the towel clumsily and stooped to snatch it up, but he was quicker, and she rose slowly and had no choice but to confront him, although she couldn't quite bring herself to meet his eyes—Damn him, she thought painfully.

'Juanita?'

'May I have that towel?' she said stiffly.

'Of course. Here.'

Their fingers brushed as she took it and her eyes lifted to his at last—to see a sort of compassionate amusement in his that told her he knew rather well what she was going through; and to make matters worse he said gravely, 'What you need—*we* need—is a long cool drink. Don't go away; I'll get it.' He indicated some chairs and a table set in the shade of a camphor laurel tree and strode towards the house.

By the time he came back, Juanita had dried herself as much as she could, donned her topaz blouse, combed her hair with her fingers and, hopefully, composed herself somewhat as she concentrated on the feel of grass beneath her feet, the dappled shade she was sitting in, the sweep of the garden and the lovely feel of being in the country.

But she wasn't helped in this exercise by the fact that he'd changed into a pair of blue swim-shorts and had a towel slung round his neck, as he placed a jug and two glasses down.

'Pimms,' he said. 'Help yourself. I really need to do this.' And so saying he discarded the towel and dived into the pool.

Juanita closed her eyes briefly then poured the Pimms, which was full of fruit and mint, and took a long draught.

Gareth Walker didn't frolic as she had. He did a couple of fast laps, floated on his back for about five minutes, then came out, didn't bother to dry himself, sat down and stretched, and reached for his glass. 'That's better. What shall we discuss today? Cheers!'

'Cheers,' Juanita echoed, but a bit wearily.

He raised an eyebrow at her. 'I should have thought you would have felt as bright as a button after your swim. You were enjoying it so much.'

'I was.'

'Until I came along and spoilt it all,' he said wryly.

'I didn't say that!'

'You looked it. You know——' he studied her assessingly '—you really need not feel self-conscious about your figure. There's a difference between slim and bony. If I were asked to describe you I would say, in fact, exquisitely slim with lovely high little breasts that remind one of buds—and the neatest set of hips I've seen in a long time. Also——' his gaze travelled downwards '—perfect, creamy thighs that a lot of women would kill for and delicate, narrow, high-arched, well-bred feet that should come as no surprise—your hands are lovely too.'

Her face had started to flame and it was still flaming as she rearranged her legs and said, 'But you weren't asked to describe me so——'

He grinned lazily. 'It's a habit. Most writers probably have it.'

'Or do they get away with sheer murder?' she said tautly.

'Oh, I don't know——'

'Why are you doing this, Mr Walker?' she broke in. 'Last night it appeared nothing could ever come to fruition between us, quote unquote.'

'I was in a more—restrained mood last night, probably,' he mused. 'Nor had I been presented with the delightful sight of you playing in the water. And I certainly hadn't witnessed the—blushing confusion being presented with me out of the blue aroused in you, and still is,' he finished softly.

'You'd be enough to make anyone blush,' she retorted.

'I can't think why,' he drawled, and drained his glass then folded his hands behind his head. 'By the way, you're singularly unmarked for someone who suffered a major accident.'

Juanita blinked. 'I can assure you I did,' she said stiffly and felt immediately foolish so she added with asperity, 'I do have a few scars as it happens but if you have a yen to check them out you're going to be disappointed.'

'But nothing major?' he queried and she realised that he was suddenly serious.

'No... I was very lucky there.'

'Good. I'm sure you deserve a bit of luck. So what's wrong with your hip?'

She looked at him warily.

'I would really like to know, Juanita,' he said quietly.

She hesitated and looked down so that her hair fell forward. 'There was damage to the tendons and ligaments. It was operated on.'

'Is there the likelihood of it coming right?'

She bit her lip. 'They say it would be a long, slow process.'

'Well, that's encouraging. OK.'

She looked up and couldn't help the query in her eyes. He smiled wryly at her. 'I meant, question time is over. Should we enjoy the last of the Pimms in——?' He stopped abruptly at the sound of a car apparently tearing up the drive then skidding to a halt on the gravel. 'Who the hell is that?'

They couldn't see the drive from the pool but they did hear someone calling his name as a car door slammed, a voice he apparently recognised, because his expression became exasperated as he stood up then called back, 'I'm at the pool, Xanthe. What the devil's going on?'

It was only moments before a vision of fair loveliness came streaking across the lawn, shedding high-heeled sandals as she came, and Gareth Walker fielded his sister as she flung herself into his arms, sobbing, 'He's ditched me! Oh, I feel as if I could die.'

'Xanthe,' he said in a hard voice, 'who has ditched you?'

Xanthe Walker raised streaming blue eyes to his. 'You know who, Gareth,' she wept. 'You told me not to have anything more to do with him but I *love* him.'

'You little fool—I presume you're talking about Damien Spencer-Hill,' her brother grated—and Juanita dropped her glass.

CHAPTER FOUR

'NO. YOU stay put, Xanthe,' Gareth warned some minutes later. They were in the kitchen where he'd carried his totally overwrought sister and was now pouring her a strong-looking brandy. He took it over to her. 'Drink this,' he said brusquely. 'And we'll have no more hysterics. You may as well sit down too,' he added to Juanita.

'I...I...'

'After all,' he went on in a hard voice as she couldn't get any words out, 'your bloody brother is the cause of all this.'

Xanthe's head swivelled round and her beautiful blue eyes stood out on stalks. 'Juanita?' she said hoarsely. 'Are you the one they all feel guilty about? What are you doing here? Has he sent a message for me?'

Juanita closed her eyes and shook her head silently and Xanthe dropped her head into her hands and started to weep again.

Gareth swore beneath his breath then went to stand beside her. 'Drink it, Popcorn.' He tilted her chin and lifted the glass to her lips. 'I did warn you, didn't I? I also really thought that by the time you got to twenty-two you'd have more sense.'

Xanthe blinked away the torrent of tears and sipped some brandy. Then she hiccuped and protested, 'I do have sense——'

'Sense? You're as mad as a March hare,' Gareth Walker said drily, and looked at Juanita. 'As for your brother, he should be shot. For a man of his experience

55

and reputation to fool around with someone as basically
naïve, not to mention as dilly as they come, as Xanthe—
well, it should be an indictable offence——'

'I'm not as dilly as they come,' Xanthe said through
more tears. 'We—he said he adored the kind of madcap
I was, anyway!'

Juanita winced.

'Well, Miss Spencer-Hill?' Gareth Walker said silkily,
but it was obvious that his sister's artless revelation had
infuriated him all the more.

Juanita narrowed her eyes. 'Well what?' she queried
coolly. 'I'm not my brother's keeper and while I feel for
anyone in—Xanthe's position, it's not my fault.'

'It isn't,' Xanthe ventured in a bleak little voice. 'I
don't think Damien and his sister get along very well.'

'So you knew nothing about this?'

Juanita compressed her lips. 'Nothing. I've never met
your sister and I don't make a practice of keeping abreast
of my brother's affairs,' she said coldly. 'What do you
imagine I would have been able to do even if I had?'

'What any right-minded person would do——'

'Oh, come on,' Juanita said impatiently, 'you're being
ridiculous——'

'What . . . what *are* you doing here, Juanita?' Xanthe
broke in, glancing anxiously from Juanita to her
brother's somewhat murderous expression.

'She's an interior decorator,' Gareth growled. 'And
as such—' he turned to Juanita '—as well as not being
your brother's keeper or willing to be much involved
with the human race at all, would you mind leaving us
alone for a while?'

Juanita stared at him and couldn't recall being more
angry in her life. But she got up and managed to say
quite smoothly, 'With pleasure, Mr Walker.'

But by the time she'd shut herself in her bedroom she was shaking with suppressed rage and had to sit on the bed for a good few minutes before it passed.

Then she changed into a pair of pewter-coloured, polished cotton trousers and a turquoise T-shirt, stared at her suitcase fixedly for a long moment, but in the end left her bedroom, bypassed the kitchen door, which was firmly shut on the murmur of voices within, and let herself out on to the side-veranda where she sat down on a bench facing the sunset.

It had cooled down a bit with the advent of dusk, and from rage her emotions had cooled to something more clinical. Such as some dark reflections on her handsome, devil-may-care brother. There was a six-year gap between herself and Damien but it hadn't only been that that had made them never be close.

During their parents' turbulent marriage and frequent separations Damien had generally stayed with their father. He had also inherited their father's tawny good looks and irresistibility to women, which Juanita resented. Not that their mother had been an angel, but perhaps because she'd always been closer to her mother Juanita had always believed her father was more to blame for their "famous open marriage", and to see Damien giving every indication of going down the same road repelled her. But the one good thing that could be said for her brother Damien, she reflected, was that for as long as she could remember he had been infatuated with cars and speed—good in the sense, she supposed, that it was something he was born with, something he had pursued relentlessly and expertly, something he hadn't been able to deny...

She grimaced at the thought and wondered yet again how *she'd* managed to be born into a family who were all geniuses in their own fields, and be so ordinary. Which led her to think of the job at hand, now going to be unbelievably difficult in these circumstances, and last, reluctantly but by no means least, of Gareth Walker.

And it crept into her mind that he must have known all along who she was—in the context that his youngest sister was having an affair he totally disapproved of, with her brother. So what's going on? she wondered. Why didn't he come out and tell me? Well, he was certainly pretty vituperative about the family, and that's obviously what it was all about, she mused, but I still can't understand why he didn't tell me. It's almost as if he's been playing some sort of... game with me, and it also explains why he kept probing for any reasons I might have for a prior dislike of him.

She narrowed her eyes and stared into the sunset quite unseeingly as it occurred to her what the game might be, particularly in the light of how he'd been this afternoon. Is it all a mock-up, she wondered, this 'curiosity' he says we share? Would he really stoop so low as to try to make me fall in love with him and then discard me to provide a taste of what he felt Xanthe was going through with Damien? As revenge? My God...

She tensed as voices floated down the veranda from an open bedroom window.

'Will you sleep now?' she heard Gareth say.

'I suppose so,' Xanthe replied disconsolately. 'I really thought he was in love with me too,' she added miserably.

'It was wishful thinking, Xanthe. The kind of mindless, self-destructive process silly little girls like you put yourself through despite all the signs. Damien Spencer-Hill is a playboy of the worst kind. Add to that the fact that he dices with death regularly for no good reason other than the thrill of it and you have a person who is constantly looking for *new* thrills. So forget him for once and for all. What about your job?'

'I . . . gave it up so I could spend more time with him.'
Juanita could just picture Xanthe's gorgeous, guilty little
face and had to shake her head as Gareth's sister continued artlessly, 'I thought it would help, we were drifting
apart—oh, Gareth, I'm so miserable! I've never felt so
desperate or confused before. I couldn't eat, I couldn't
sleep.'

'OK,' he said with a certain amount of rough sym-
pathy, 'the recriminations are over for the time being.
On one condition—are you listening to me, Popcorn?'

'Yes, Gareth.' This was said obediently.

'You're going to stay here with me for a while
and——'

'But——'

'But me no buts, my dear, foolish sister; you have no
choice. You have no job and therefore no money and I
don't propose to lend you any.'

'That's—Gareth, that's cruel!'

'Is it?' he said drily. 'Who gave you that Ford Capri
for your twenty-first birthday?'

'Well, you did but I mean——'

'Xanthe.'

A short silence. Then, 'All right, Gareth. But what
will I do here? I'll be so bored!'

'No, you won't. You can help Wendy until Mrs Spicer
gets back. It'll do you good.'

Xanthe groaned. Then she said in a brighter voice,
'Perhaps I can help Damien's sister while she's here?'

'I wouldn't count on it,' Gareth Walker said. 'I haven't
made up my mind whether she'll be staying.'

The birdsong outside Juanita's window the next morning
was almost deafening.

She woke, consulted her alarm clock, sighed and contemplated one of the disadvantages of living in the

country—over and above the disadvantage of living in this particular house in the country, she reflected. Where one couldn't be sure if one was about to be fired or, if one wasn't, what enlivening events would occur today.

She'd decided to take a walk last night after overhearing Gareth and Xanthe and by the time she'd got back Wendy and the twins had returned and dinner was ready.

Wendy had raised an expressive eyebrow at her as if she were one of the family and said, 'Bit of drama. There always is when Xanthe's around. Have you met her?'

'Yes. When she arrived.'

'Well, she's not feeling very well apparently, so Gareth has given her a sleeping-pill. And he's taken his meal into the study and said he's not to be disturbed unless Xanthe needs him—he's not in a very good mood.' She'd grimaced.

'Oh,' Juanita had murmured, then smiled at Wendy. 'Never mind. I've been wanting to ask you about the lemon chicken last night. I'd love to have the recipe.'

And that was how she'd come to spend a pleasant evening playing snakes and ladders with the twins before they were consigned to bed, then helping Wendy clean up the kitchen while they discussed their favourite recipes. And she'd taken herself to bed the same time as Wendy. Gareth had not emerged from his study.

As she lay in bed listening to the birds, though, on another wonderful, clear morning, she recalled the decision she'd come to the previous evening—and decided to give it some more thought. It was never wise to act in anger, after all, or in pique. There were also some imponderables to be considered. *If* Gareth Walker had been playing a rather deadly little game of revenge on her brother, through her, how would it be affected if he sacked her?

It would still rebound on me, she answered herself. Both ways I'd be the scapegoat because I could lose my job. And he could be angry enough or enough of a louse not to care which Spencer-Hill he hurts, or how, so long as he gets one of us. I feel rather like the fly and the spider... Of course, the big question is that *if*.

And I suppose that all boils down, she mused, to whether I believe these sort of spontaneous attractions do occur, *so* very spontaneously...

She broke off her reflections there rather ruefully but then continued stubbornly. All right, forget about me, although do bear in mind what happened to Laura Hennessey—what about him?

But that proved almost impossible to resolve and the result of all this introspection was, she discovered, a particularly strong impulse not to be made a fool of for whatever reason or by any man. And if he deserves the benefit of the doubt, he can always prove himself, can't he? Don't forget how he greeted you, as if all Spencer-Hills were anathema to him, and then changed somewhat—there had to be a reason for it, she told herself.

With these fighting words she got up, showered, donned a pair of emerald tracksuit bottoms in a fine parachute silk and a white T-shirt, tied her hair back simply, made her bed, gathered her notes and headed for the kitchen.

There was no one about so she made herself some tea then set out for the drawing-room where she worked quietly and peacefully for nearly an hour until she heard the unmistakable sounds of a household coming to life.

Rebecca and Steven were her first visitors—they'd come looking for her when they'd discovered her bedroom empty and they were full of curiosity about what she was doing, and then delight when she drew quick sketches of them. They finally ran off chattering loudly and excitedly, only to be caught by Wendy and admonished for making so much noise. Wendy herself was the next to pop in to tell her she'd made friends for life of the twins but not to allow them to bother her.

Then there was a lull until she felt the back of her neck prickling and looked up to see Gareth Walker watching her from the doorway.

'Oh! Good morning.' She'd been photographing the bow window, twin of the one in the dining-room, and she put the camera down and simply waited for his re-action. He wore jeans, no shirt or shoes, he hadn't shaved, his hair was hanging in his eyes and he looked thoroughly irritable as he leant his broad shoulders against the door-frame and his deep blue gaze slid over her.

'Good morning. I didn't really expect to see you,' he answered at length.

'You didn't?' She opened her eyes at him. 'Why not?'

'I thought you might be angry enough last night to do a bunk.'

Juanita shrugged. 'I was certainly angry.' She picked up a sample book of fabrics she'd got from the car. 'But a job is a job. The proportions of this room are won-derful, aren't they?'

He wasted not so much as a glance at the proportions she was admiring or the fabrics she was running through her fingers. He said instead, 'And it never even crossed your mind to hightail it back to town and wash your hands of us?'

Juanita smiled faintly and refused to allow her mind to dwell on the fact that his skin was smooth and tanned, his chest sprinkled with gold hair, and that, despite being ill-humoured and dishevelled, he was incredibly at-tractive. 'It did, but your house got me in, Mr Walker,'

she replied gravely. 'I woke up and found that out-
weighed all else—you don't mind, do you?'

He narrowed his eyes and said nothing.

'Mr Walker,' she prompted finally.

'I do——' But he got no further as the twins re-
appeared, bearing their portraits and still excited.

'Look at this, Gareth!' Steven jumped up and down
beside him. 'Can she ever draw!'

Gareth squinted down.

'And this is me!' Rebecca pushed hers into his hands.

'A thoroughly disreputable pair if ever I've seen one,
not to mention noisy at the crack of dawn,' he
commented.

'It's no use showing Gareth *anything* before he's had
breakfast, Steven,' Rebecca chided. 'Or even trying to
talk to him. Will you draw our dog for us later, Juanita?
If we're good and don't bother you while you're working
and don't fight?'

'Certainly,' Juanita said.

They scampered off.

Juanita turned away to hide her amusement.

'As I was saying, Miss Spencer-Hill——' Gareth
Walker remarked after a moment, but Wendy chose that
moment to breeze in.

'Breakfast's ready,' she announced. 'I wish all your
guests were like Juanita, by the way, Gareth. We had
such a nice evening last night and she always helps.
Um . . . will I wake Xanthe or leave her be?'

Gareth regarded her with even less favour than he'd
bestowed on the twins. Then he said, 'We'll be with you
shortly, Wendy. Leave Xanthe.'

Juanita waited a moment as Wendy's footsteps retreated. Then she murmured, 'As you were saying,
Mr Walker?'

'What the hell is this?' he countered as he straightened and closed the door. 'A plan to take over my entire household?'

'Not at all,' she responded calmly, and had to laugh, but inwardly, at the sheer murderous quality of his look. 'Why would I want to do that?'

'You tell me,' he grated ironically. 'And you may be prepared to gloss over the matter of your bloody brother but I'm not!'

'All right,' she said coolly. 'Let's discuss it. I don't hold much brief for my brother generally, believe me, but I venture to think that your sister is not exactly a model of common sense and it's not only my brother you would have to worry about.'

'And I venture to think,' he said acidly, 'that you are far too *full* of common sense, Miss Spencer-Hill. You're also an early riser and obviously at your best at this ungodly hour, all brushed and bright-eyed and bushy-tailed—and altogether too much for me to live with.' His blue eyes smouldered.

If I weren't so angry with him deep down, I'd be enjoying this, Juanita thought. 'You don't have to live with me, precisely,' she pointed out. 'You're very welcome to ignore me completely, Mr Walker. I promise you I won't take umbrage in the slightest.'

He ground his teeth.

'I might also be of some slight value to you in the matter of Xanthe,' she said carefully then.

'How?'

'Well, for one thing, I could point out to her that Damien has been faithful to no one for long as far as I'm aware, other than his long-standing affair with speed and cars. Perhaps that's why—I don't know.' She gestured. 'Er—does Xanthe . . . w-work or anything?'

An interrogating blue glance flew her way and she knew her stammer had done it. The first she'd suffered this morning. Surely he couldn't know it was due to nerves because she felt slightly dishonest about what she'd overheard the night before, though? All the same her heart beat a little faster.

He said then in a clipped voice, 'No. She gave up her job to spend more time with him. And jobs and Xanthe aren't that easy to pair together.'

'Then—mightn't she be interested in the redecorating of the house?'

He closed his eyes briefly and said reverently, 'God alone knows what we'd end up with. A cross between a seraglio and a south sea island paradise. Xanthe has some way-out ideas.'

'What about one guest bedroom? The one she uses. You could always keep it as a talking-point.' She spread her hands. 'I just thought while she's getting over this it might give her something to do.'

'And it didn't cross your mind to think that while there was a Spencer-Hill in the house it would keep Damien fresh in her mind?' he enquired witheringly.

'I could be wrong,' Juanita said evenly, 'but it might only take another personable young man to cross her path for you to be going through this all over again.'

She saw the inescapable logic of this strike home, not that it afforded him any pleasure. He set his teeth then said bitterly, 'What a prospect. In the good old days I could have locked her up in a convent.'

Juanita smiled genuinely. 'She'd probably have escaped. I can't help thinking that girls like Xanthe...' she hesitated '...well, that their biggest problem is an overflowingly loving nature, and that's no sin. The right person may yet come along; don't despair.'

Several expressions chased through his eyes and it struck Juanita that she might be taking unfair advantage of a person who was obviously never at his best before breakfast. Not that she hadn't believed what she'd said, nor that she wouldn't do her level best to help Xanthe get over Damien if she got the opportunity, but it had to be galling to be presented with all this good sense at your worst time of the day, and by someone you perceived as an enemy, moreover. How would he respond? she wondered. Groggily, like someone on the ropes, or nastily...?

'Unlike you, of course, Juanita,' he said softly, although his expression mocked her. 'There doesn't seem to be an excess of love flowing through you, does there?'

She flinched inwardly and cautioned herself against ever believing again that she was taking unfair advantage of Gareth Walker. She also said coldly, 'You may think what you like. You might as well also tell me whether you want me to go on with this job or not. Whether...' she paused and glanced at him proudly ' ...the mere fact of my name and this unfortunate coincidence is sufficient cause for firing me.'

He stared at her narrowly and for the first time left the doorway and padded towards her. 'Unfortunate or otherwise,' he said roughly, 'don't get too arrogant with me, Juanita. Until I sign a contract I'm under no obligation to Bluemoon. So, bearing that in mind, you may proceed with your interior decorating.' He stopped beside her and took the sample book from her. 'I don't like any of these, by the way.'

Sheer effort of will made Juanita restrain herself from telling him he was behaving like a spoilt child, let alone hitting him. But the effort left her speechless, and anyway, in the moments before she lowered her lashes to hide what was in her eyes, their gazes clashed rather like steel upon steel.

'I thought so,' he murmured. 'That the sweetness and light you began this confrontation with was a bit of an act. Would you care to tell me exactly what you're playing at, Juanita?'

'I'd rather *you*——' She broke off abruptly.

'What?'

'Nothing!'

'Oh, yes, there is,' he drawled. 'Let's try this for size. Are you in the unenviable position of thinking you hate me but—wanting me at the same time?'

She gasped. 'How can you *say* that——?'

'I just did. Although why you should hate me so much is beyond me——'

'It *would* be!' she flashed. 'And I suppose it appears perfectly natural that I should . . . sh-should want you—of *all* the——'

'Perfectly,' he said with a faint, dry little smile, and took her chin lightly in his hand. 'Nor is it unnatural anyway.'

'Forgive me, but I have to think you have an unnatural, not to mention unhealthy ego. You're . . . you're pulling this all out of thin air!'

'Am I?' He released her chin and put his hands round her waist but made no further move other than to still the convulsive way she shuddered. 'Don't panic,' he advised rather grimly. 'If you believed I go in for rape you'd have left long ago. But let's examine this thin air as well as what's unnatural and unhealthy. It was none of those things yesterday when you came out of the pool and got so awfully—confused. It was simply your body responding to mine and it was all heightened because you were wet and not wearing much; you had been swimming with a lot of grace and pleasure—and it affected us both.'

Juanita could only stare up at him, her lips parted, breathing agitatedly.

'But it was also more,' he said flatly. 'I've seen hundreds of pretty girls in pools but once you've got to know someone you either go on or it all goes away.' He smiled though not with his eyes. 'The way they talk, what they say and how it reflects what they think, how they manage their lives—some of those things can do it in about two minutes flat—I'm sure you've noticed the same about men?'

She licked her lips but didn't reply.

'The point I'm making,' he said with a sudden glint of devilry in his eyes, 'is that it hasn't gone away for either of us yet.'

Juanita found her tongue. 'You were all set to fire me not so long ago!'

'I may have been.' His lips twisted rather wryly. 'It wouldn't have stopped me—thinking about you, Juanita. Do you know the kind of things that come to my mind?' He went on without giving her a chance to reply. 'That you're well named. There's something quite Spanish about your colouring—and the way those dark eyes flash from time to time. You also have incredibly long lashes. And I can imagine lace, thick, heavy lace looking wonderful against your bare skin. The contrast of textures, rough and so—smooth would be quite something.' He stared into her eyes for a long moment then looked down and moved his hands slightly on her waist. 'And then there's your waist,' he said barely audibly, 'so small, yet you're a good height for me.' And he looked into her eyes again.

She didn't know how he did it but that almost somnolent blue gaze now, and the warmth of his hands on her, seemed to dispense with her T-shirt and bra and in a moment of awful clarity she saw herself in her mind's eye wearing nothing but lace against her skin for him, a mantilla perhaps, draped lightly over her breasts, and she could even feel the scratchiness of it against her nipples...

'Oh...' she whispered, and closed her eyes, going hot and cold again and starting to tremble as that lovely feeling started to build once again, as well as another image—of him, shirtless as he was now and bending over her, pulling the lace aside, lifting her so her breasts were touching the hard wall of his chest... 'No.' Her lashes jerked up, a dew of sweat beaded her brow and she strained against his hands. 'How do you *do* this...?'

He looked at her curiously sombrely. 'It's mutual, my dear Juanita, as I've tried to tell you before. And I could prove it to you if you cared to witness me taking a cold shower—sorry,' he said as her eyes widened, and he released her abruptly; 'I didn't mean to shock your virginal sensibilities so much.' And he turned away and strode over to the window.

Juanita stared at his back and licked her lips. Then she frowned bewilderedly because it struck her that his sombreness had been quite genuine and if he was playing games with her, why would he look like that—as if what was happening to them was as discomfiting to him as it was to her?

She opened her mouth but that was when the door opened and Xanthe looked in. 'Gareth? Oh, there you are!' She came in and her brother turned from the window and rubbed the blue shadows on his jaw ruefully.

'So I am. How do you feel?'

Xanthe smiled palely. 'Better.' But a spark of interest lit her eyes as they came to rest on Juanita. Then she glanced at Gareth questioningly.

'Miss Spencer-Hill is staying for the time being, Xanthe,' he said rather drily. 'She's also—I wonder if she's a mind-reader?—suggested you might like to help her. Within reason, of course, but you could do your own thing with your own room.'

CHAPTER FIVE

'DO YOU mind me helping you, Juanita?'

Juanita had moved to the dining-room when Xanthe entered during the afternoon. 'No.' She looked up and smiled. 'How are you feeling?'

Xanthe pouted. Then she said honestly, 'Rather foolish. Sad. I suppose I should be angry with Damien but...' She shrugged and tears came to her eyes. 'I really thought this was the big love of my life.'

'I'm afraid quite a few girls have felt the same way.'

Xanthe digested this then she looked at Juanita curiously. 'You two hardly have anything to do with each other, you and Damien. Why is that?'

'We were never close. And quite different personalities. He was always the bright one while I was a bit like the ugly duckling.' She shrugged.

'And now you disapprove of him thoroughly, I suppose,' Xanthe said flatly.

Juanita sighed inwardly. It was obvious that any criticism of Damien was not going to be well received at this stage. 'Not thoroughly, no,' she said with a slight smile. 'He is still my brother.'

Xanthe sighed heavily and openly. 'Men are hard to understand, aren't they?'

'I have to agree with you,' Juanita responded with some irony, thinking of Xanthe's brother. 'But there is one—er—way of dealing with them.'

'What's that?'

'Let them do the chasing.'

71

Xanthe wrinkled her brow. 'You could end up an old maid like that and anyway, in this enlightened age all that's old hat, surely!'

'I'm not so sure,' Juanita said slowly. 'I suspect some things never change and one of them could be that men like to be the hunters. They're more—stimulated, if you like, by having to pursue a quarry. They also don't like to think we can be impervious to them and it spurs them on, and when they do finally win you they feel they have some sort of a prize.'

Xanthe looked intrigued and then doubtful. 'I may not be made like that.'

'Oh, well, it was just a thought. Should we have a look at your room?'

'This dog,' Juanita said late in the afternoon when she'd packed up for the day. 'Where do I find him?'

Rebecca took her hand. 'Down at the stables. He's not allowed up at the house.'

'Why is that?'

'He does a lot of wrong things,' Steven said with a grimace. 'He digs holes in the garden, he frightens the life out of people who come to visit although he only wants to be friendly and he's only a puppy really, but after he jumped up on the minister's wife and pushed her into the fountain Gareth said enough was enough.'

'Not that Gareth likes the minister's wife,' Rebecca put in. 'He says she's an interfering old busybody and no one's told her ministers' wives don't do the rounds any more, but all the same...' Rebecca eyed her twin and they burst into peals of laughter. 'It was very funny,' Rebecca said at last. 'Gareth had to climb into the pond himself to get her out. She's quite a fat lady and was she ever mad! She even swore at him. He told her he'd never liked her more but that only made her madder.'

'I see. Er——' they were crossing the garden by this time '—I'm a little scared of dogs myself and——'

'Oh, he won't hurt you!' Steven assured her. ''Specially not when we're there. Although he does guard the stables.' This was added proudly.

'Does he roam around the grounds?' Juanita asked with a frown as she thought of the awful risk she might have been taking by walking as she had the previous evening.

'No. There's a fence round the stables. See, we go through this gate.'

She relaxed a bit. 'What's his name?'

'Westminster. We asked Gareth to help us choose a name. He said if he was any judge he was not only going to grow to the size of a house but a house of parliament, no less. He was right.'

They'd come to the gate by this time, but much as she tried to will herself through it Juanita couldn't do it. 'Kids,' she said ruefully, 'I cannot tell a lie—I'm too scared to meet Westminster unless he's tied up. Is he?'

'Oh, no, not yet but——'

'Then why don't I wait here, on this side of the fence with the gate closed while you get him—and keep him on the other side? In the meantime,' she added rapidly as they both opened their mouths to protest, 'I'll start sketching his namesake.' And with a few bold strokes she began to draw Big Ben in one corner of her pad.

It was a few minutes before anyone appeared and then it was Gareth as well as the twins, with a huge amber Great Dane lolloping along beside them.

Juanita sighed. She hadn't laid eyes on Gareth Walker since Xanthe had interrupted them earlier but of course it was inevitable that she would. Nor had she been able to sort through the tangle of emotions their encounter had aroused, but worse than that she was now unable to still the slight colour that came to her cheeks, or the *frisson* that seemed to attack her nerve-ends.

But he gave no sign of anything untoward as he called, 'Fear not, Miss Spencer-Hill. I've tamed the beast somewhat since the reverend's lady was consigned to a watery place. Sit,' he added to Westminster over his shoulder.

Westminster sat obligingly although his attention was eagerly focused on the stranger he perceived through the fence, and he barked by way of greeting.

Juanita winced as the sound reverberated. 'Thank you but I think I can see all I need from the safety of where I am,' she called back.

Gareth Walker strolled to the fence and put one leather-shod foot on the bottom bar. He was again wearing jodhpurs with a yellow T-shirt this time. Westminster made to come forward too but at a glance changed his mind and stayed seated. His master said, 'He's really a most amiable dog, you know, and, were I to introduce you formally, you would have a friend for life.' His blue eyes glinted with amusement.

'Possibly,' Juanita conceded. 'But it might just be the one friend I'm going to have to do without.'

'I do feel, however, that, seeing as this place is going to be your home from home for a while——' it was a glint of sheer wickedness that she saw in his eyes now '—it would not only be wise but beneficial to make friends with Westminster. Do you have a fear of dogs in general or just this one?' he queried gravely.

Juanita shot him a speaking look as Rebecca and Steven gathered at the fence interestedly. 'Nine people out of ten would have a fear of this dog,' she ventured.

'Which just shows how wrong the majority can be. Come,' he said and held out his hand to her, 'one can't be a coward about everything and I promise I won't allow any harm to befall you anyway.'

A spark lit her own eyes but she hesitated as she saw the undoubted curiosity with which the twins were eyeing them—and stiffened her spine.

'That wasn't so bad, was it?'

'No.' Juanita watched as the twins gambolled about with Westminster utterly fearlessly and saw how gentle the dog was with them. 'No.'

'He's only a big kid himself.'

'Does that mean he's going to grow even bigger?'

'I hope not,' Gareth said ruefully. 'Are you going to bear his image in mind or sketch him here? There's a log you could sit on over there.'

'I—w-what are you going to do?' Juanita bit her lip.

'I'll stay with you.'

She grimaced. 'Thank you. I suppose you think I'm an awful fool,' she said, and blushed as she realised she was still holding his hand. But at least she'd been able to resist the urge to throw herself into his arms. She pulled her hand free and sat down on the log.

'Not at all.' He sat down beside her. 'A lot of people are scared of dogs, and you with more cause than most probably, because you lack some mobility—and I don't mean to offend you by saying that,' he added quietly.

She looked into his eyes and they were sober but she couldn't forget the gibe about being a coward about *everything* . . . so she shrugged, said, 'Thanks,' briefly, and began to sketch.

'Can you talk while you're drawing?' he asked after a time.

'Oh, yes.'

'You've obviously inherited some of your mother's talent.'

'Not a lot.'

'All the same, that's a nearly perfect likeness of Westminster.' He stared down at her pad.

'Likeness, yes, but I lack the—touch of genius to imbue what I draw with a soul of its own. And I lack the imagination to create anything other than likenesses.'

'I'm not sure that I agree with you,' he said slowly. 'You've just captured a huge, eager, over-friendly, clumsy dog on paper. That's Westminster in other words.'

Juanita smiled slightly. 'No. I mean, yes, it is but I wouldn't be at all surprised if most young Great Danes were huge, eager, et cetera, et cetera.'

'Be that as it may,' he persisted, 'you've got the spirit.'

'You're very kind,' Juanita murmured and looked up to see him frowning down at her. 'W-why are you looking at me like that?'

He narrowed his eyes then said reflectively, 'It *can't* have been easy growing up in the shadow of such talented parents.'

Juanita stopped sketching for a moment then her pencil wandered to a spare corner of the pad and she began again. 'I guess we all have things that are difficult to grow up with.'

He looked wry. 'Of course. Take Xanthe for example. She's not only the youngest of seven but there was a bit of a gap between her and the next one up. So in some ways she was rather like an only child and, in any case, seven kids are enough to exhaust you, probably. What ever——' he gestured '—our parents often took the line of least resistance with her. For which we're now reaping the rewards—oh, I don't blame them entirely.' He grimaced. 'Faced with Xanthe I seem pretty helpless myself.'

'What about her older sisters?'

'All paragons of virtue,' he said drily. 'Well, not really but over their salad days and preoccupied with families as well as spread far and wide around the continent.'

'So it's all left to you?'

'More or less.' He was silent for a time then he surprised her by saying softly, 'So you have a sense of humour, Juanita? I wondered about that.'

'What? Oh.' She saw he was looking down at her pad again. What she'd drawn was a caricature of herself sitting awkwardly on the fence staring with a look of comical horror towards the larger sketch of Westminster. She looked up and their eyes locked but once again she was saved as the twins bounded up. And the dog.

'Pat him,' Gareth said quietly as Rebecca and Steven enthused and laughed over her drawing and showed it to Westminster.

She did, tentatively, and was rewarded by a joyful bark. 'OK, kids, take him away,' Gareth said. 'Shall we walk back?' he added to Juanita.

'It must be like having a ready-made family,' Juanita said once they were through the gate, and mainly for something to say, but immediately she remembered his dead wife and child, and winced.

He merely shrugged and adapted his long stride to suit hers. 'They're good kids. You seem to get along with them pretty well yourself.'

They walked in silence for a few minutes and she took the time to look around and breathe deeply. The sun was setting and the wonderful, wild garden was alive with birdsong again. Against the backdrop of a pale tangerine sky, smoke was curling lazily from one chimney—Wendy's mother would not be parted from her Aga cooker apparently. It came to Juanita that as a child she'd always dreamt of living somewhere like this, of being involved with trees and plants and animals instead

of the inner city, although luxurious series of flats she'd
lived in . . .

'What are you thinking?'

She glanced across at him, startled. 'That I l-like it
here, that's all.'

'In spite of me.' His lips twisted. 'I take it that you've
forgiven me for last night—and this morning?'

Juanita raised her eyebrows. 'I think I'll reserve
judgement on that.'

'Well said.' He smiled briefly and stopped as they came
to a stand of pampas grass. 'You're—calmer than I
thought you would be. About this morning.'

'Am I?' She laughed a little hollowly. 'I can't imagine
why—well, no, I can,' she amended, and said honestly,
'These little *interludes* we have seem to have an unreal
quality about them. Had you noticed?'

'No,' he replied promptly. 'You don't think that might
be wishful thinking?'

Juanita tightened her lips and shot him a fiery look.
'On the subject of wishful thinking, trying to make me
believe I'm a coward is not going to help your cause
either, Mr Walker.'

'I stand reproved, Miss Spencer-Hill,' he replied
gravely. 'Perhaps that was a slightly cheap shot. But when
you are—to a certain extent—fumbling around in the
dark, you tend to try all the shots in the book. I apologise
for my mixed metaphors.'

Juanita assumed an expression of marvelling inno-
cence. 'And I thought I was such an open book to you!
As a student of human nature, not to mention a man
on the——' She stopped.

'Prowl?' he supplied lazily and his teeth gleamed white
against his tan. 'Now was that a shot in the dark or
something expressly calculated to wound me?'

'If the hat fits, wear it,' she said tartly.

'Well, I've thought of a couple of hats that might fit you, Juanita,' he said blandly. 'Unawakened was one; that you could be one of those mentally sterile, passionless females who despite the promise of their looks can never come to terms with their sexuality was another——' He broke off as Juanita paled. 'What now?' he said after a moment.

'*Nothing*. I'm going in,' she said through her teeth.

'I don't believe you are frigid, incidentally,' he said, and put a hand on her arm, but she shook it off.

'Don't try to stop me, Gareth Walker,' she warned fiercely, 'unless you'd like to be attacked in a most vulnerable spot by a walking stick. And don't you dare lay your hands on me ever again!'

He stared at her intently through the gathering gloom. 'It seems I might have hit a nerve. Were *you* beginning to wonder if you were frigid, Juanita?'

'I was not—oh, you're just impossible!'

'That's better,' he said, still watching her intently.

'*What* is? No, don't bother, I don't want to know.' She turned away.

'You've got some colour back.' He started to walk beside her. 'I thought you were going to faint for a moment.'

'I'm not the fainting type,' she retorted.

'Good. Well——' they approached the back porch '—perhaps we need a drink. How did you get on with Xanthe today?'

Juanita cast him a speaking look, tried *to* speak, but nothing would be said other than an indecipherable stammer.

'Yes, definitely a drink,' he mused, reaching for her hand. 'For what it's worth, I apologise for anything I may have said that hurt you.'

She tried to pull away angrily but Wendy popped her head out of the kitchen door and said urgently, 'Is that you, Gareth? Xanthe's really upset.'

Xanthe was face down on her bed sobbing her heart out but she lifted her head to say in throbbing, watery accents, 'If that's you, Gareth, go away! I know what you're going to say—that I'm a fool; well, maybe I am but I just can't help it and I feel like dying!'

'Listen, Popcorn——' Gareth sat down on the side of his sister's bed and lifted a tress of her fair, curly hair '—do you think I've never made a fool of myself? I've never told you this but I once fell in love with a woman who was ten years older than me—I was about your age actually and I used to... well, I used to write poetry to her, really lovesick stuff, and I used to dream and plan and——'

Wendy and Juanita melted away and closed the door softly.

'Did he, I wonder?' Juanita mused out aloud, then bit her lip.

'We might never know—it couldn't have been his wife, she was younger, but so long as Xanthe believes him it might help.' Wendy pulled a face. 'So it's all over some man, this. I wondered.'

'Not just some man but my brother—by a most unfortunate coincidence,' Juanita said drily.

'Oh, dear.'

'Yes. Apparently he's ditched Xanthe.'

'Never mind. Gareth will sort her out. He's the only one who ever could.'

They reached the kitchen and Juanita looked thoughtfully at Wendy. 'He never talks about his wife, does he? And there don't seem to be any pictures or anything. You . . . tend to forget he ever had one,' she said slowly.

Wendy grimaced. 'You're right. I've never liked to ask—perhaps she was the one great love of his life and he can't bear to be reminded. I wonder how many people are going to want dinner tonight?' she added with a rueful frown.

In the event they all sat down at the kitchen table and although Xanthe said little she managed to eat and then she got a long phone call from a girlfriend which seemed to brighten her up a bit.

Juanita quietly helped Wendy clear up the kitchen and Gareth took himself off to his study looking rather grim. He had also been quiet and preoccupied during dinner.

Juanita decided to work but it was somewhat abstractedly and she finally took herself to bed and came to a decision—she would go back to town the next morning.

She presented herself to Gareth in his study shortly after nine o'clock, neatly dressed in the fawn skirt she'd worn the night of Wendy's dinner and a short-sleeved cotton-knit top the colour of wild raspberries. Her lipstick and low-heeled suede shoes were the same colour.

He looked up from his word processor and raised an eyebrow. 'You look as if you're leaving us, Juanita,' he murmured wryly.

'Only temporarily. Before I make too many plans for your house I thought I should assure myself that the kind of fabrics and so on that I have in mind are in stock.'

'Couldn't you do that on the telephone?'

'It also helps to see them in the flesh, so to speak.'

He regarded her thoughtfully. 'Well, when would we have the honour of expecting you back?'

Juanita clenched one hand but said coolly, 'In a couple of days.'

'I see. OK. Have fun,' he drawled.

Juanita looked away then left the room without replying. But she knew that he knew this was partly an excuse to get away and she felt both angry and embarrassed.

Neither did either of those two emotions leave her over the next two days as she roamed fabric and furniture warehouses—and couldn't get Gareth Walker out of her mind. But the worst times were when she was alone at night in her Lavender Bay flat. She couldn't believe how he occupied her mind and how the thought of him filled her with a sense of turbulent restlessness and an astonishingly new awareness of herself. Astonishing in the recollection of how her body responded to him and the knowledge that she'd lived her life to this point in a pair of blinkers regarding her sensual capacity. Deliberately, she wondered, since the accident at least and for a reason that few people knew about? She stared into the darkness starkly then forced her mind to change course. To what, for example, dismayed her most—that a man who could infuriate her, patronise her, who sometimes played it all as a rather deadly little game, a man she'd known so briefly, to make matters worse, could have this effect on her.

I should despise him, she thought miserably as she tossed in bed one night. There are times when I *do*. But none of that changes...the fact that I can't stop thinking about him! And thinking about things like his shoulders and his skin and his hands...

She closed her eyes and felt the colour mounting to her cheeks—and buried her face in the pillow abruptly.

*   *   *

Nothing seemed to have changed much when she arrived back after three days.

Wendy and the twins greeted her as a long-lost friend, Xanthe looked relieved to see her but Gareth merely smiled faintly and enquired whether seeing things in the flesh had been as helpful as she'd hoped.

She could have killed him, she found, at the same time as her heart started to beat heavily just at the sight of him, standing tall and nonchalant at the hall table and going through the mail which had arrived just before she had, and was of about equal interest apparently as he flipped envelopes aside lazily and failed to be moved to open any of them.

She closed herself into her bedroom that night, after working at a furious pace during the day trying to draw all the threads of her ideas together with what she'd seen in the warehouses, but knew with a sense of desolation that she wouldn't sleep.

She moved to the window and breathed in the scented darkness and forced herself to remember the suspicions she'd harboured towards Gareth Walker. But even though all her nerves seemed to be at jangle-point it was, she realised, back in his house, a new dilemma that was as much the cause of her turmoil now as anything else. It was as if she was face to face with a question along the lines of, Who is this man? What is his true face? A concerned, compassionate brother? There seemed no doubt about it. Xanthe was definitely calmer, and dinner with the twins and Wendy had been a pleasant meal with Gareth subtly in charge to make it so. Then there was Wendy and the twins, and it was impossible to doubt their genuine affection for a man who had not only done a lot for them but was genuinely fond of them in turn. In other words, she thought, there were other sides to

Gareth Walker... And there's the wife he never talks about and the child he lost...

She sighed and turned away from the window and contemplated her bed. But no amount of looking at it or willing herself to feel sleepy had the desired effect so she decided to have a bath and hope for the best.

Indeed she did feel more relaxed after a long soak in the antiquated tub—there was nothing wrong with the water, it was hot and plentiful—and she decided that a nightcap of some kind would just about do the trick. But she hesitated at her door for a few moments then decided to take the plunge. There were no sounds anywhere and her bedroom was on the other side of the house to Gareth's study and the master bedroom, and close to the kitchen, which appeared to be in darkness. She tightened the sash of her violet velvet robe and sallied forth.

The kitchen was not completely in darkness, she discovered as she opened the door. One light burned at the far end of the large room and the very person she had hoped to avoid was sitting at the table drinking tea.

He turned his head and subjected her to a glance that held no surprise and very little interest. Just a slightly ironic quirk of an eyebrow that for some reason annoyed her...

'I thought there was no one about,' she said, still hesitating in the doorway, and was more annoyed to hear herself sounding defensive.

'You were wrong. Is that a problem?'

'N-no. I came to get a nightcap, that's all. To help me sleep,' she added.

'Be my guest,' he murmured. 'I'm having tea, but there's Milo, cocoa or you could be even more adventurous and have whisky and milk—one of Mrs Spicer's favourite sedatives. Only in times of great need, of course. Mrs Spicer is the soul of propriety normally.'

'How fortunate,' Juanita murmured, and forced herself to advance into the kitchen. To do anything else now would be slightly ridiculous, after all.

'It is, isn't it?' He sat back in his chair and flexed his shoulders wearily. 'I just wish she were here at the moment.'

Juanita fetched a cup and saucer and poured herself tea. 'I think Wendy's coping admirably by the look of things.'

'Wendy is. But were her mother in residence I could take Xanthe away for a while.'

'Ah. Do you think that would help?'

'Obviously,' he said irritably. 'I wouldn't be thinking of it otherwise. Don't you?'

'Temporarily it might. But, until something else or *someone* else engages her interest, perhaps only time will help.'

'I hope to God you're right,' he said abruptly and shoved his hands into his jeans pockets moodily.

'How—how is the book going?'

'What book?' he said sardonically.

'The one you're working on.'

'It's not going at all,' he said flatly.

'Ah.' Juanita sipped her tea. 'That must make things difficult.'

'Not only that.' He shot her a pure black look of scathing intensity. 'The fact that we are sitting here uttering platitudes to each other is not doing my state of mind the least bit of good either,' he said cuttingly.

For some reason Juanita refused to be perturbed. 'I do understand,' she said calmly. 'My mother goes through this often.'

'What,' he enquired with deep sarcasm, 'does your mother do about it?'

'Admits that a padded cell is what she needs so that she can go off her rocker privately and without doing herself or anyone any damage. What do you do about it?'

He pushed his chair back, stood up restlessly and prowled aimlessly around for a minute or two. Then he said drily and with a significant look at her robe, her loose hair, 'That doesn't seem to be the answer either at this precise moment, assuming there was any possibility of it anyway.'

Juanita grimaced. 'Has this ever happened to you before?'

'No.'

'Could you...' she paused carefully '...be hankering for some permanence in your life in that regard?'

'I don't know. Could I? It sounds more like what women hanker for,' he replied frankly. 'How about you? You obviously don't seem to be hankering for anything in that regard despite being a woman.' His glance was sardonic.

This time she refused to take offence although she thought drily that any probings of that nature were obviously going to be blocked. So be it... 'Not yet,' she said honestly. 'Well, I suppose I have wondered what it would be like to be married and wondered—er—who...'

'And what did you come up with in your wonderings?'

Juanita was silent, thinking, until he said mockingly, 'Someone who is the antithesis of me?'

She couldn't help the tinge of colour that stole up her throat.

He smiled, a rather savage little smile.

'What makes you think that?' she demanded defiantly, then coloured more hotly.

He shrugged and looked genuinely amused. 'I've got the feeling your ideal man would probably be intellectual, certainly not overtly physical, gentle, perhaps a bit of a dreamer, quiet and kind——'

'What's wrong with th——?' She broke off and bit her lip and marvelled that he could be so acute.

He looked at her intently, then shrugged. 'Nothing. It's just not necessarily what you need.'

'Surely only a very wise man or an utter fool,' she said tartly, 'would presume that on such a short acquaintance?'

'Well, I don't claim to be *exceptionally* wise but I'm not a fool either and I merely said that—what I was *trying* to get across——' his irritation and impatience returned '—was that one should not base one's judgement of men, or women or children or whatever, on the shortcomings of one's family.'

Juanita blinked. 'I thought it was you I was—w-well...'

He grimaced. 'OK, me as well.' His lips quirked. 'But it interests me that you should pick someone quite different from your brother or your father as the kind of man you'd like to marry.'

Juanita stared at him.

'Listen,' he said with a sort of rough compassion, 'there has to be some reason for it and unless you're prepared to tell me what it is I can only guess.'

'Reason for what?' she said on a suddenly agitated breath.

'Why you are the way you are, Juanita Spencer-Hill,' he said drily. 'But don't imagine I'm going to prise it from you; I think I'll go to bed instead and——'

'*No.*' Juanita stood up, all the turmoil boiling up within her and causing her to throw caution to the winds. 'You can't say things like that and then—go to bed! What in the world gives you the right to tell me that goodness and kindness and r-r——' she put the back of her hand against her mouth '—r-r...I can't *say* it...' She closed her eyes and sat down again, bent her head over her teacup and ran her fingers despairingly through her loose hair.

It was the slightest sound that alerted her, through her inner tears of inexplicable frustration, to the fact that he'd sat down beside her. She swallowed and sat up. 'Sorry,' she said stonily.

'For what?'

'For getting all emotional.'

'Who cares? I don't——'

'Thanks!' She looked fleetingly bitter.

'I meant that I don't regard it as a——' he gestured '—lowering of one's standards or stupidly female or anything like that. I think it's a good idea to get emotional now and then, in fact. Too *much* restraint can be as bad as too much hysteria.'

'That's the word I was trying to say,' she said, and sniffed.

There was silence for about a minute. Then he said, 'Do you know there's a full moon tonight?'

'Is there?'

'Mmm. As a kid I used to love sitting on the back step watching it—would you care to join me there now?'

'I——'

'It's not cold.'

'All...all right.'

'I'll bring us a drink.'

He brought two balloon glasses of liqueur brandy and a cushion for her, as well as a mohair rug—just in case it turned chilly, he said.

And they sat in an oddly companionable silence for a while, sipping their brandy and watching the moon create a silvery fairyland of the garden. Until she said,

'I don't usually talk about these things but I do also firmly believe one can't blame one's parents for—I mean, you must come to a stage when you shouldn't blame anyone for the way you are.'

'Go on,' he said quietly.

'Well, for all their flamboyance, they loved me and the real problem was that I was so different. I spent my childhood longing to live somewhere like this; I desperately wanted us all to be together and to be able to be quiet together but at the same time I longed to be brilliant like my father or beautiful and talented like my mother, and then there was Damien, so good at just about everything—it was like being torn in two; do you know what I mean? Anyway I've already told you all this,' she muttered, feeling suddenly guilty.

'It doesn't matter; go on.'

'Well, then to compound matters I had the accident and I felt even more of a freak, but I also began to feel angry. The way they carried on started to seem trivial. And exhausting.'

'And therein lay the seeds of what was to become a disenchantment with them,' Gareth said soberly. 'So you turned away from them, you cut your name in half and that's when they all started to feel guilty?'

'I didn't realise they had until Xanthe said it,' Juanita replied ruefully. 'Anyway, I thought, lately, that I'd got to that stage where one understands we're all made differently and it's no good blaming your parents for everything—I have. Got to that stage, I mean. But yes, quietness and kindness and restraint—perhaps I should drink more brandy—and a lot of the things they *aren't*, are high on my list of priorities, probably as a legacy of it all; but that I just can't seem to help.'

He was silent, staring at his glass cradled in his hand.

'Doesn't that make any sense to you?' she said at last.

'Of course. But it might be wiser to try to keep a more open mind.'

Juanita digested this and was tempted to ask him rather drily if he meant in relation to himself, but was stopped by the thought that throughout this exchange, at least, there'd been a quality of disinterest about him, as if he was viewing her problems as a spectator. She grimaced and asked him something else—to do of course with the one thing he didn't know about her and something that was occupying her mind more and more. 'Is it *so* obvious what I'm going through? I hadn't even realised myself—I mean, I thought I was sailing along on a rather even keel, enjoying my job, my independence, not really languishing over the lack of a man in my life,' she said, trying to sound lightly wry.

'It's obvious,' he said slowly, 'that you step backwards pretty smartly from men.'

'There's a reason for that——' She stopped abruptly, unable to believe what she'd been a hair's breadth away from telling him. She swallowed. 'I...w-well, I've had a couple of disagreeable experiences.' Which was all too true as well, unfortunately.

'Tell me.'

'I've been made aware...' she paused '...that I should be grateful for any man's attention and that I should reciprocate by leaping into bed with them, because of my...disabilities.'

'I see.'

'I wonder,' she said coolly.

'Are you accusing me of this?'

She shrugged.

'Thank you.'

She shrugged again and sipped her brandy. 'Believe me, it has happened. And when things happen like that more than once they can't really be coincidences, can they?'

'No, but then all cats may look grey at night yet they certainly aren't.' She stiffened at the allusion but with a grave glance he added, 'That one strolling across the lawn right now, for example, is a ginger tabby.'

She smiled faintly; she couldn't help herself. 'I take your point. A residual wariness, however, is probably only human.'

'Probably,' he agreed.

'Well, that's me,' she said with an attempt at flippancy. 'What about you?'

'What about me?'

'Funnily enough, you were more—outwardly—disturbed than I was this evening. I'm not quite sure how we came to change roles but you were definitely disillusioned and down in the dumps.' Her lips quirked.

He stretched his long legs out and sighed. 'So I was.'

She waited a while then said, 'You even indicated you may have gone off women.'

'Heaven forbid,' he replied wryly. 'Did I say that?'

'Not in so many words but it's what you gave me to understand—that's how all this started,' she reminded him.

'Ah, yes,' he murmured. 'Might I be hankering for some permanence in my life? To tell you the truth, Juanita, I don't know what the hell I'm hankering for, and if I do manage to get this book going I might discover I'm not—lacking anything. Writer's block can be a thoroughly destabilising, maddening process.'

'Perhaps Xanthe's problems haven't helped,' she suggested.

His lips twisted. 'Much as I would love to blame Xanthe and——'

'My bloody brother.'

'As you say. But I've lived through Xanthe's traumas before—no, this is quite... new. I mean, everyone goes through it periodically but this is different.'

'Worse than normal? I mean, my mother goes through something similar with every portrait she paints.'

'No wonder your father—be that as it may,' he said with a swift laughing look so she was unable to take offence. 'Uh... yes, worse than normal. And I'll tell you——' he sat upright suddenly and frowned '—what didn't help, which should amuse you. That know-all woman with her "literature with a capital L" opinions.'

'Who—you mean Laura?'

'None other, bless her cold little heart.'

A laugh trembled on Juanita's lips. 'But you said——'

'I may have said a lot of things,' he broke in with an arrogantly cutting look, 'but I'm now trying to write Booker Prize kind of stuff—no wonder it's not going well!' he marvelled.

'You mean you've only just realised this?' Juanita stared at him wide-eyed.

'*Yes*,' he said through his teeth.

'Is... that such a bad thing?'

'For me it's a disaster.'

'Why?'

'Because,' he said impatiently, 'I'm not that sort of writer. I'm no Graham Greene, I'm a formula writer, and they don't win Booker Prizes.'

'I see,' Juanita said neutrally.

He swore, drained his glass and stared into the moonlight looking thoroughly disgusted.

'You did say,' she ventured tentatively, 'that you reserved the right to write what you like—it seems strange that Laura Hennessey should have got under your defences like this.'

'Not strange at all,' he said grimly. 'Some women make a pastime of—reducing men in stature as much as they can, which is a much more kindly way of putting it than what I had in mind to say.'

'Oh, come now——'

'Don't "come now" me——'

'You're being ridiculous, though,' she said coldly.

'Am I? I wonder.'

'You are,' she assured him. 'I would say that, just as most people believe they have one book in them at least, most writers would love to win a Booker Prize or the Pulitzer or the Nobel——'

'I have never, in my entire career, visualised myself winning the Nobel, believe me,' he said precisely and witheringly.

There was a short silence.

'But you might be right,' he added thoughtfully then and in far less aggressive and outraged tones than before. 'That's what I'm hankering for—some glory. Dear me. Why didn't I see this creeping up?'

Juanita could help herself no longer. She laughed softly.

He cocked an eyebrow at her. 'What does that mean?'

'I don't know. Actually, I thought it was rather sweet, the way you admitted that.'

'Sweet?' His expression defied description for a moment, then they were laughing together and he put an arm round her shoulder and it felt like the most natural thing in the world. 'How come you're so intuitive?' he queried.

'Maybe we both are. You because you're a student of human nature as a writer even if you're not Booker Prize material and me because—when you've spent a lot of time sitting on the sidelines of life, you observe a lot.'

'Maybe. But it's a criminal waste for you to go on sitting on the sidelines, Juanita,' he said quietly.

She went very still and felt foolish tears prick her eyelids. 'I try not to,' she said huskily.

'Look at me. Are you crying?'

'N-no.' But she sniffed.

He drew her closer and tilted her face towards his. 'There's a motto, an acronym, that comes to mind, I don't know why but it's peculiarly appropriate.' He observed the glitter of tears in her dark eyes. 'Know what K.I.S.S. stands for?' he added gently.

Her lips parted and she frowned. '*No*, but——'

'It stands for "Keep It Simple, Stupid". With that in mind, and the stupid refers to me, of course, could I kiss you very simply and only as a tribute to someone who is rather brave, after all?'

'Oh, I——'

He did. With utter simplicity that was quite stunning nevertheless, and Juanita, who had never particularly enjoyed being kissed before, was unable to resist. She wondered why and thought that it might be because he didn't attempt to hold her any more closely than he already was and his lips were cool and firm and he didn't attempt to part hers at all. So that was all it was really— a sort of salute, but as he drew away a tide of something she had no control over rose up within her and she made a strange little sound and touched her fingertips to his face.

'Juanita,' he said very quietly after a moment of utter stillness, and covered her fingers with his own, 'you——'

'Could regret this—I know,' she whispered, 'but I'll never know until I've tried, will I? You see, I've never enjoyed being kissed. Perhaps you could be my teacher, that's all.'

'Things don't always work that way,' he said with a touch of grimness, staring down at her upturned face.

She blushed and closed her eyes. 'Of course, s-sorry——'

She thought he swore beneath his breath and she was ready to die a little but then he said roughly, 'Don't look like that.' And gathered her into his arms.

They sat like that for a time and, incredibly, despite her embarrassment, she found herself sorting through all her impressions—such as that being held the way she was was rather lovely and oddly relaxing and it emphasised a consciousness of her body and made her feel desirable. It also drew her attention to his, and she couldn't still a small tremor that she identified as a kind of joy that he should be so beautifully made, lean and strong... It was when she realised this that her lashes sank, then she opened her eyes to stare up into his.

And her lips parted in what could only be an invitation. She thought he hesitated briefly and started to wince but then his mouth closed on hers and before long they were kissing extremely intimately, their bodies resting together now, and she had her hands on his back, stroking and feeling. And when he lifted her on to his lap it was a wonderful feeling to rest her head on his shoulder until he started to kiss her again.

The only thing they didn't do was talk—it seemed entirely unnecessary.

But quite necessary for a third party they had no idea was observing them until Xanthe said in high, overwrought tones from just inside the kitchen door, 'Gareth! How could you? After all you've said to me. Oh, I don't believe this!'

Gareth lifted his head, his hands momentarily hardening on Juanita, who froze.

'Xanthe,' he said in a hard, clipped voice, 'this is *not* the same thing.'

'Not the same thing! You told me you didn't really know Damien's sister from a bar of soap! If you must know I think it's disgusting, and don't think I'll ever allow you to preach to *me* again. As for what *she* told me—she obviously doesn't practise what she preaches either!' And with a toss of her curls she retreated with a flounce.

Juanita came out of her frozen daze and attempted to free herself.

'No——'

'Yes,' she whispered distraughtly. 'She's right!'

'She isn't—don't you go all dumb and dizzy on me.' He looked at her sardonically.

'Oh!' Juanita said on an indrawn breath, and, gathering herself, managed to tear herself away and she fled inside as fast as she was able.

CHAPTER SIX

IT WAS a long, lonely night.

Juanita locked herself into her bedroom but it was an unnecessary gesture. No one attempted to visit her. And she lay in the dark searching distraughtly for some explanation of her behaviour, some clue as to why she *was* so devastatingly attracted to Gareth Walker, she of all people and so much so—there really was little to choose between her and Xanthe.

It was an intensely mortifying thought, but perhaps even more difficult to cope with was what he would be thinking of her—and not necessarily her confused repudiation.

She twisted uncomfortably and stared into the darkness, remembering what he'd said before he had really started to kiss her as well as his dispassionate dissection of her earlier, and grimaced painfully. She also remembered the morning after Xanthe had arrived home, although it seemed like a lifetime away, and how, just before Xanthe had interrupted them yet again, she'd got the feeling that he had been as unsatisfied as she had about the state of affairs between them. But why did he kiss me, she wondered, and touched her fingertips to her lips, when he didn't really want to, other than very briefly? Did he think he could teach me as I suggested? Or did I just put him in an impossible situation?

She sighed unhappily, and she'd resolved nothing as dawn crept upon the landscape, and to make matters worse she then fell heavily asleep for a couple of hours

and missed all the drama that took place in the early
hours.

'Say that again?' Juanita requested.

Wendy glanced at her as she sat at the kitchen nursing
a mug of coffee with the evidence of a sleepless night
written on her face in the form of deep shadows beneath
her eyes. 'Xanthe snuck off very early this morning and
left a note for Gareth saying that she wasn't going to let
him interfere in her life ever again. Which put him into
a real rage and he drove off to try and find her.'

'D-did she say where she was going?' Juanita asked,
her eyes huge and anxious now.

'*He* said if she thought she was going back to throw
herself at—well, at your brother——' Wendy grimaced
'—she was mistaken.'

Juanita closed her eyes.

'Mum, I need to know where Damien *is*. I want to speak
to him urgently.' Juanita clenched her hand around the
phone until the knuckles showed white.

'Darling, this is unusual. I didn't think you and
Damien communicated much at all.'

'We don't,' Juanita replied tersely.

'So what's come up? Do tell me.'

'I can't. Do you have any idea?'

'Let's see . . . Isn't the Adelaide Grand Prix coming up
in a few weeks? It's generally round Melbourne Cup
time, isn't it—or is it the Gold Coast Indy Grand Prix
I'm thinking of? Your father would probably know.'

'Do you have any idea where Dad is?'

Her mother chuckled down the line. 'He's always been
a hard man to pin down, hasn't he? Uh . . .'

'Don't bother, Mum,' Juanita said wearily. 'I should have thought of checking the Grand Prix circuit first——'

'Now that's probably the best idea but if Damien does get in touch I'll tell him you're *burning* to talk to him. How's the job going? It seems an age since I saw you, darling. How are you?'

'Fine,' Juanita lied. 'I—I'll come and see you soon, Mum.'

'Do! I know I've never been a clucky sort of mother but—— '

'Mum, I have to go but I will pop in soon, promise! Bye now!'

It was the Adelaide Grand Prix coming up in a few weeks, she discovered, but after exhaustive enquiries with the company who sponsored her brother Damien she was only able to establish that he was in Adelaide somewhere but no one could be more specific than that.

And the only ray of hope about that is, if Xanthe does have in mind trying to track Damien down, she might be as frustrated as I am, Juanita thought.

With that in mind she tried to settle down to some work but found herself roaming the house trying to imprint as much of it as she could on her mind instead of concentrating more specifically as she'd planned to. The reason for her doing this only became plain at lunch...

'That was Gareth.' Wendy put the phone down. 'He's found her. They'll be back in time for dinner.'

'Oh,' Juanita said slowly and pushed her plate away. 'For sure?'

'Yep. Steven, you're supposed to eat butter on bread, not the other way round! And go easy on the jam.'

'This isn't a lot of butter and jam, Wendy,' Steven protested.

'Yes, it is,' Rebecca said severely. 'Remember what Mum says. When she was a girl she was only allowed to have either bread and butter or bread and jam, not both.'

'And both in moderation,' Wendy murmured, removing the jam jar.

Steven looked aggrievedly at his sisters in turn and then over their shoulders as if the spectre of his absent mother hovered. 'I wish Gareth was here,' he muttered. 'He understands about growing boys!'

For some reason this simple sentiment moved Juanita curiously, and brought her to a decision. 'Well, I should be getting back to town again, Wendy,' she said as casually as she was able. 'I would have stayed another night to keep you company but if Gareth and Xanthe are on their way back...' She moved her hands. 'You don't need me,' she finished brightly.

Wendy looked faintly surprised. 'But you'll be back?'

Juanita smiled at her. 'This job is going to take a while. You could be sick of the sight of me!'

All three protested vigorously and in unison that they wouldn't and she felt a strange feeling of warmth clutch at her heart-strings and then a sense of bewilderment...

'Does Gareth know you're going?' Wendy queried.

'No,' she said honestly after a moment. 'We didn't really get a chance to discuss it but I'll leave a note for him. They could probably do without having a stranger in the house for a few days,' she added lightly, and changed the subject.

Wendy made no more of it and when Juanita drove away about an hour later they all waved her off—So why do I feel bad about this? she asked herself. Why should I feel a sense of family for three people I barely know and as if I'm running away at the same time? Am I? Perhaps...

*   *   *

'So this is where you work.'

Juanita looked up suddenly three days later to see Gareth Walker lounging in the doorway of her cramped little office.

'Y-yes. Hello.' She rose awkwardly and couldn't think of a thing further to say, as well as being acutely conscious that she was blushing hotly.

He watched her idly for a long moment—the colour in her cheeks, the lovely ivory linen and lace blouse she wore with a full, gathered, mint-green skirt, the matching mint ribbon tying her hair back. Then he said rather drily, 'Hello, Juanita. What are you working on, as a matter of interest?'

'Y-your h-house, of course,' she stammered, glancing down at the sketches spread over the desk before her.

'I'm relieved to hear you say so. In lieu of any communication from you other than that stilted, extremely unforthcoming little note you left me, I was beginning to wonder whether you'd decided to drop my house right out of your calculations. What time do you finish work?'

Juanita stared at him but he simply outstared her in a way that she suddenly was no match for and she dropped her gaze and said tonelessly, 'I was planning to work until about six but——'

'Good. I'll pick you up then.'

She looked up, arrested. 'Why?'

He smiled, but it was a cool, faint twisting of his lips. 'I thought I told you once before, Juanita, that I'm a great believer in plain speaking—or were you planning to file that kiss away as something unreal?'

Her eyes widened and she tried to speak but no words came.

'So I thought we could discuss it over dinner,' he murmured. 'Don't worry about having to change; you look fine as you are.' He straightened.

'N-no... w-wait... there's nothing to discuss...'

'I'm afraid there is,' he said briefly. Then added with irony, 'Unless you'd like me to believe you really do practise what you preach regarding men and how one should let them do the chasing...'

'What you accused me of earlier,' Juanita said several hours later, in a restaurant of his choosing, after a short, silent taxi ride to it from work, 'is ridiculous.' They'd barely been seated and the drinks he'd ordered had not yet arrived but she'd been rehearsing this speech for hours—and alternately fuming and feeling cold with fright.

He raised an eyebrow at her. 'Go on?'

'Well—I gather Xanthe repeated something I said to *her*...'

'She did. How you advised her to handle men actually was what she repeated and it's not hard to see that from her point of view it made you look rather dubious.'

The unfairness of this all but took Juanita's breath away. 'You said—you *told* her it wasn't the same thing at all!' she protested angrily, then stopped abruptly.

He grimaced. 'I haven't changed my mind.'

'Then why—are you doing this?' She stared at him.

'Because I got the distinct impression only shock tactics were going to work.' He sat back and waited while their drinks were served. 'But just as a matter of interest, why did you kiss me the way you did, Juanita? And then run?' He lay back in his chair and sipped his drink.

He wore a beautifully cut tweed jacket, an open-necked cream shirt and well-pressed twill trousers, and was better dressed than she'd ever seen him—there were few women in the restaurant who hadn't secretively glanced his way. Juanita opened her mouth, closed it as she wondered whether these were also shock tactics, and changed the subject slightly. 'How is Xanthe?' She took a long swallow of her drink.

'She's in Perth,' he said briefly, his eyes registering this evasion, however.

'Well, that's a fair way from Adelaide...' The words popped out before she could stop them.

'Where Damien is? Yes. I consigned her to her eldest sister.'

'She went willingly?'

'I wouldn't put it quite like that.' His eyes were hard. 'She only went because she saw a picture in the paper of your brother with another girl hanging around his neck—a girl she knew, who had been dying to supplant her, apparently. But at least she went with some anger in her heart against him.'

'I'm sorry,' Juanita said inadequately. 'I...I spoke to Damien myself and tried to tell him what kind of havoc he'd caused. He——' she put her glass down and twisted her hands '—well, that doesn't matter now, does it?'

'No. But what was he? Surprised? Defensive?'

'Both,' Juanita admitted. 'He said he'd told Xanthe he wasn't looking for a commitment—I don't believe that absolves him from anything,' she said straightly, '—so——'

'I wasn't going to take issue with you.' He looked briefly amused for the first time since he'd appeared at her office doorway. 'So you've fallen out with your brother?'

She shrugged. 'We were never close.'

He picked up the menu and studied it. 'That leaves us, then. May I recommend the Châteaubriand? It's their speciality.'

'All...all right,' she said uncertainly.

'You're wondering what I'm going to add about us?'

She winced. 'I don't think there's a lot to s-say on the subject,' she murmured. 'I——' She stopped as the waiter came to take their order.

'You...?' He shot her an interrogative glance as the waiter departed.

Juanita sighed. 'I can't understand why you're taking it all so seriously,' she said perplexedly then. 'You must be so used to having women——' She stopped, picked up her drink and looked away frustratedly.

'Does that mean to say you really class me with your brother, perhaps your father?'

She coloured and took another swallow of her drink.

'Juanita?'

'No...I don't know,' she said barely audibly.

He grimaced. 'And how do you see yourself?'

'What do you mean?'

His lips twisted and his eyes glinted wickedly for a moment. 'As an older version of Xanthe, for example?'

'N-no.'

'As a seductress who gets her prey firmly in her sights, gives them a taste of her then retreats?'

'No.' Juanita put her glass down with a snap and eyed him angrily.

He considered her silently for a moment then said quite soberly, 'As someone who is attracted to a man against her will and—afraid of it and where it will lead?'

Juanita went still and lowered her lashes.

'Juanita?'

'Is—that's not your problem,' she said barely audibly and with tears pricking her eyelids.

'Why not?'

She steeled herself and banished her ridiculous tears. 'Because——' she looked up at last '—I've got the feeling now that I'm in the same league as Xanthe—even Wendy and the twins. Look,' she said with sudden decision, 'I have to be honest and tell you that...whatever happened to me I decided was—well, a bit crazy——' she grimaced '—and that I was better off not letting it get out of hand; something l-like that,' she said with a despairing smile. 'I do hope you can understand.'

He was looking at her so steadily as she finished her awkward little speech that she couldn't help catching her breath and then saying rather wildly, 'I know you didn't really want to kiss me——'

'I did as a matter of fact——'

'Let me finish!' she commanded. 'I know that a lot of what got me in was the house, the garden, the kids, the sense of *family*, even if it wasn't real. I know that originally you were angry about Xanthe and Damien and might have seen me as a way of getting revenge—I'm not stupid!' she said scathingly. 'I also know that the last person you need is someone like me, so could we just forget about it all——?'

'*Revenge*?' he said softly.

But she chose to ignore that and proceeded jerkily, 'And get on with...*something*. Dinner, seeing as you're so determined to buy it for me!'

'All right.' He shifted in his chair but his eyes were inimical. 'Here it comes, and while you may eat in peace I'm not letting you go,' he warned, 'until you tell me why you're the last person I need and what on earth you mean about being in the same league as Rebecca and Steven—and of course this new theory of revenge. But eat now——' he looked at her drily '—and we'll continue this debate over coffee. Where do you live?'

Juanita closed her eyes, then said defeatedly, 'Just across the water. Lavender Bay.'

The restaurant was in the historic Rocks area of Sydney and it had a terrace where one could overlook the harbour, the bridge and the Opera House. They'd eaten inside but Gareth had decided they should have their coffee outside after forcing her, with no display of strength at all, she thought bitterly, to respond to his amiable flow of conversation during their meal.

It was a partly fine, starry night but a bright sliver of moon was silvering a build-up of clouds yet making magical reflections on the water. Juanita looked out over the harbour and found her flow of small talk drying up— or perhaps it was because he had suddenly become silent and thoughtful.

Until he said, 'Did you drive your car to work? I forgot to ask.'

'No. It's easier to get a bus to Chatswood.'

'Lavender Bay,' he mused. 'A flat?'

'Yes. Bought for me by my mother and father.' She grimaced.

'You don't like Lavender Bay?'

'I like it very much, and my flat. I love the view and being able to get on a ferry and come across here, it's nice to be close to Kirribilli, the Opera House—I would just rather have earnt it myself.'

'What about your hankerings for the country and *my* house?' he queried.

She felt herself colour but said staunchly, 'I thought I'd told you how it was one of my childhood dreams.'

'So you did.'

'Doesn't that explain it?' She looked at him tautly.

He shrugged uncommunicatively. 'What about why you'd be the last person for me, then and why you feel an affinity with Rebecca and Steven?'

Juanita licked her lips. 'They go together,' she said finally. 'I think you're basically a kind person——'

'I hesitate to contradict you so early in your piece,' he said drily, 'but there are times when I'm not kind at all.'

'All the same,' Juanita persevered, 'you care a lot about Xanthe and are very good to three fatherless children. And, while I'm not fatherless, for other reasons...' she hesitated '...I think I fit into...' She stopped and shrugged. 'I think you might feel sorry for me; let's not beat about the bush!'

'Why?'

Juanita stared at him.

'Why what?'

'Should I feel sorry for you?'

Her gaze became withering. 'Isn't it obvious?'

'Because you limp and stammer—it doesn't matter in the slightest to me.'

Juanita opened her mouth then closed it. 'It must,' she said very quietly in the end. 'It would one day.'

'I think these things have become blown out of proportion in your mind, Juanita,' he said after a moment's thought. 'It's a very slight limp and a very occasional stammer unless you're nervous, and it even has a quality of—charm. I've also wondered whether your limp mightn't...have something to do with a lack of confidence.'

Her eyes widened. 'Are you saying it's psychosomatic?'

He shrugged. 'Why not treat it as such for a while and see what happens? *Is* there any medical reason for it now?'

'I...' she bit her lip '...I haven't been to the doctor for a long time. My mother keeps urging me to but I got so sick of it all.'

'It would not be unknown,' he said slowly, 'or indeed anything other than quite human to——'

'Hide behind a walking stick?'

His gaze held hers until the bitter little glint in her eye faded. 'I was going to say—to never want to see a doctor or hospital again.'

She looked away but said, 'I know you mean well. I do know that——'

'Good, because I do. And I could also be quite wrong so I think you *should* go back to your doctor and discuss it with him. Here endeth that lesson. Drink your coffee.' He looked upwards. 'We could be in for a shower.'

'Oh.' She looked confused. 'What will we do?'

'What would you like to do?'

She coloured. 'I meant about transport. You didn't bring your car up.'

'I did. That was one of my reasons for coming. It appears to have a major gremlin in the carburettor that they could only sort out temporarily in Mittagong so I've put it in to the agents up here.'

'I see. Well,' Juanita said brightly, 'I can get a ferry home so don't worry about me. You're probably staying on this side of the harbour anyway.'

'I'm not. I'll see you home on the ferry, if that's what you would like, and then get a cab from there.'

Juanita hesitated, glanced at him and switched her gaze away as she realised her heart was suddenly beating oddly, and she felt hurt because he hadn't come solely to see her, as well as curiously dissatisfied as if this encounter was ending up in the air with nothing resolved—but what did she want resolved? she wondered. His acceptance that she wasn't for him? No, damn it, she thought, but that makes me even crazier than I believed. So why don't I look at it from another angle...?

'Juanita?'

She blinked. 'Yes?'

He didn't answer immediately but studied her in the dim light, and it made her angrier and hurt her in a new way that he looked . . . She closed her eyes but the image of Gareth Walker was imprinted in her mind, and it made her pulses hammer and her mouth go dry to realise how deeply he affected her. How she didn't want him to be sitting across from her looking austere and uncommunicative, and not be able to know what he was thinking—still not to know how he really saw her . . . As someone he could fall in love with or someone who'd come into his life unexpectedly and, because of the way she was, someone he, belatedly, didn't want to hurt?

'What are you thinking, Juanita?'

Her lashes flew up as she went inexplicably from pain to anger. 'If you must know I'm wondering whether I need my head read,' she said tartly. 'Who's to say? I mean, I know nothing about you other than that you're kind to kids and cripples——'

'Juanita——'

'Well, I don't,' she flung at him. 'You could still be an absolute bastard where women are concerned. And you think you have the right to accuse me of . . . of leading men on!'

'So you're wondering,' he said, quite lazily 'if you're getting your knickers in a knot over nothing?'

She jumped up and all but ran off—but she was gasping for breath when she came to the ferry terminal, and limping heavily, and she didn't have the strength to resist when his hand closed on her arm and he steered her aboard the ferry.

It was a short journey across Sydney Harbour from Circular Quay to Lavender Bay, and, as they'd done in the taxi to the restaurant, Juanita and Gareth Walker made it in silence. The clouds had now obscured the moon, the air was heavy with humidity and lightning was starting to zigzag across the sky, reflecting eerily in the dark water. It occurred to Juanita that it was about to rain any minute—a not very acute observation, but then her whole state of mind felt dull and heavy and she wasn't even particularly conscious of the man beside her.

It did rain. Just as they stepped off the ferry, the heavens opened up in tune with a mighty clap of thunder and within seconds she was drenched.

'Which way?' he said urgently into her ear.

'Up these stairs; it's this block,' she gasped, and gasped again as he picked her up in his arms.

'You can't——'

'Shut up and lie still,' he ordered. 'I can and I will.'

They stood in her hallway, dripping and both breathing heavily as she fumbled for the light. She found it at last and they stared at each other.

His lips twisted and he reached out and squeezed her hair. 'You look half drowned.'

'I feel half drowned—so do you. Your jacket could be ruined.'

He shrugged. 'It shouldn't be—sheep get wet all the time. Is this as far as I'm to get? I don't imagine it will be too easy to get a taxi until this abates a bit.'

She bit her lip then stiffened her spine. 'After what you said to me I wouldn't take anything for granted, Mr Walker!'

'Gareth,' he murmured. 'And I apologise. I have an unfortunate facility for trading insults for insults.'

Juanita turned on her heel and walked into her lounge, lighting lamps as she went, and she reverted to the subject of taxis. 'That doesn't mean to say we couldn't order one, but in the meantime the laundry's through there if you'd like to dry off a bit; I'll use the bathroom.'

When she came back he was standing at the wide windows overlooking the harbour, watching the lightning. He'd removed his jacket and shoes, towel-dried his hair and placed a towel thoughtfully over one of her leather chairs.

'I like your place,' he said without turning, and she wondered how he'd known she was there.

'Thanks.' Her walls and carpet were pale grey, her leather suite a beautiful pale jacaranda-blue and there were touches of dusty-pink and sherbet-green in lampshades, and it was airy and spacious, designed to make the most of the wonderful harbour view. 'How did you get on with a taxi?'

'Not for at least an hour.' He turned at last and allowed his blue gaze to drift wryly over her. She'd exchanged her sodden clothes for a pair of white trousers and a black blouse. Her hair was loose and still damp but brushed and orderly and she had a pair of very soft silver kid flatties on her feet. 'Still—immaculate,' he murmured.

She raised an eyebrow. 'I wouldn't call it that exactly. Do sit down. Would you like a drink? Or coffee?'

He shook his head. 'Nothing, thank you.' And sat down on the towel-covered chair.

Juanita hesitated then sat down opposite him. Apart from the sounds of the storm there was utter silence for about a minute. Then she swore beneath her breath and glared at him. 'This is ridiculous.'

He smiled faintly. 'We could always discuss the weather.' He paused. 'Unless you'd like a detailed account of my love-life to date instead?'

'I would not,' she said frostily.

'I thought it might help you to know me better,' he drawled.

'Why would I want to know anyone who can't understand my...my reservations better?' she countered.

He sat forward and clasped his hands between his knees. 'Unfortunately, it's never that simple, Juanita,' he said drily. 'Should we try to get a couple of things straight? We—laid eyes on each other and some kind of charge appeared to trigger itself. A charge you resisted rather properly and I——' he moved his shoulders but his eyes were narrowed and intent as they rested on her face '—was prompted to respond to out of—let's say a certain amount of pure male pique.'

Her lips parted and she blinked.

He smiled briefly. 'I'd never before met a woman who was so flatly determined to be unimpressed—or to *resist* being impressed, and at times, I have to admit, it brought out the worst in me. But the fact remains right from the beginning—well, if you really want to know, I thought— "Another member of this blasted family", I thought, to be precise,' he said evenly, his blue gaze curiously ironic, 'another flighty and no doubt wayward but oh, so stunning Spencer-Hill.'

Juanita closed her eyes. Then she said bitterly, 'So I was right.'

'You haven't let me finish,' he pointed out.

'What's there to finish? I couldn't understand why you hadn't come right out and said . . . something about Damien and Xanthe.'

'Well, I'll tell you if you'll allow me to get a word in edgeways.' He looked at her with one eyebrow raised sardonically. 'I said nothing because I'd cut up so rough with Xanthe on the subject of Damien Spencer-Hill that she had promised me she would break it off. I hesitated to believe her but when he went overseas and she stayed put I gave her the benefit of the doubt. Then I got immersed in this book that's proving so hard to write and it eluded me that he was back and it was all on again. In fact I had no idea it was until Xanthe appeared the other day. She——' he grimaced '—had taken some pains to hide it from me. So...' he paused '...while I may have initially—lumped you in with the rest of your family when you first landed on my doorstep, I had no idea Xanthe was in the process of getting ditched. But for the record, while I may have some faults, getting to some guy through his sister on account of *my* sister is not one of them. I would far rather punch him on the jaw,' he said grimly.

Juanita turned away from the look in his eyes and believed him.

'What's left?' he queried after a moment. 'I don't view you as an object of charity, I don't have any deep dark plans of revenge, so you really have nothing left but your desirability to fall back on, Juanita.'

'Do you mean...?' She looked back then away again and licked her lips.

His lips twisted. 'Yes. I mean your desirability from my point of view.'

'I...look,' she said suddenly, 'I wanted to say this to you the other morning, the morning I got up early and you...and you—well, do you know the morning I mean?'

'The one I had to take a cold shower—yes.' He didn't look even faintly amused.

'Well, what I wanted to say then was that—if I didn't like this ultra-spontaneous mutual attraction or whatever it is, you didn't like it much either.'

He stared at her.

She went on bravely, 'And I still think so. Even if you...might have wanted to kiss me—properly, I mean— I couldn't help feeling that you thought you shouldn't. Which was why all those other things I've thought seemed to make sense. But now I can't help wondering if it might have something to do with your...wife.' There, it was out at last, the question that had been at the back of her mind, getting buried often but still there.

'You're right.'

Her lips parted. 'So she was the love of your life and you can't forget her?' she whispered.

He smiled, but not with his eyes. 'Nine years is a long time to be in love with a memory. And we'd only been married for two years when—it happened. Not that that means anything.' He looked at his hands. 'What my real problem is—I'm not the kind of man a girl like you should fall in love with. I know saying that is akin to closing the stable door after the horse has bolted—I mean——' his eyes narrowed as she blushed '—that I'm more to blame than anyone that it should have ever entered your head, but unfortunately it's true.'

'Why?'

'Because it's not my intention to marry again, Juanita,' he said quietly, his eyes holding hers steadily.

'*Why*?' She said it again and winced.

'Because I'm lousy marriage material, that's why, and that's what I came up to town to tell you.'

'You were unhappy in your marriage?' she whispered.

He stood up and walked over to the window. 'I found the lack of independence hard.' He stopped then turned to her squarely. 'And Linda became unhappy, probably with a lot more cause. I wasn't home much, although we lived in Rome mostly, I wasn't there when our son was born—nor, for that matter, through much of what must have been a difficult time for her. She was a journalist too and had been used to roaming the world, so pregnancy and being housebound wasn't easy. Nor was I there when they got—wiped out one dark, wet, miserable night.'

'But you've given up that lifestyle—I...I mean...' Juanita bit her lip. 'Not that we're talking about marriage.'

He stared into her eyes and she got the feeling that he could see into her soul—and that she'd given herself away totally... 'Not really—given it up,' he said gently then. 'I still get the wanderlust and I go away in other ways too. It wouldn't have been so easy for Xanthe to deceive me otherwise. And there are periods when I'm impossible to live with.'

'A lot of women must have that problem, though,' Juanita said confusedly. 'Being relegated into second place to their husband's careers—but do you think you're being a hundred per cent honest?'

He lifted an eyebrow at her. 'I'm not?'

She frowned. 'Monogamy may just not suit you—as it doesn't Damien, apparently.'

'If you think I go through women the way your brother Damien does,' he said with a cutting little edge, 'you're wrong. Are you trying to tell me it isn't in me to be faithful?'

'I don't know,' she said painfully. She looked at her hands clenched in her lap then up at him. 'Are you trying to tell me we could have an affair but not to have any further expectations?'

Their eyes locked. 'No,' he said at last, 'I'm trying to tell you an affair with me is the last thing you need; but what, above all, I'm trying to tell you is that it's not because you're unworthy of it in any way—I'm the one who is.'

CHAPTER SEVEN

'DON'T you think I should have some say in it?' Juanita said after an age.

'No——' But he stopped as she stood up abruptly, looking visibly distressed. 'You're angry,' he said quietly then. 'You have every right to be.'

'I don't know what I am,' she said, hugging herself distraughtly. 'But I can't help feeling if it weren't *me*, if this had happened between you and someone else, you wouldn't be saying...what you have.'

'Juanita—perhaps.'

'Oh,' she whispered, and turned away from him.

'But not for any of the reasons you're imagining. Only because I wouldn't want you to find love and then discover—it couldn't be fulfilled.'

'Then you shouldn't——' she licked the tears that ran to her lips '—you shouldn't have...even tonight...' She couldn't go on.

'I know I shouldn't have done all sorts of things, but it was a gradual process—realising that I could only hurt you. You told me yourself how much a home and a sense of permanence meant to you, but by that stage even I could see it. You told me how much kindness and restraint meant to you, and even though I mocked it—well, it was probably mostly because I knew I couldn't give it to you. But even tonight, and forever,' he said, 'I wanted you to know that one man thought more of you than—just someone to go to bed with, however much I would like to do that too. I'm sorry,' he said very quietly, 'but there didn't seem to be any other way to get it across.'

She put her hands to her face for a moment. 'What if I were to tell you,' she said indistinctly then, 'that I would never expect you or any man to marry me anyway?'

'Juanita,' he said harshly, 'don't. Don't ever rate yourself second-best like that; I don't, believe me.'

She looked at him white-faced. The tears had stopped but she brushed her face with her wrists. And she opened her mouth but stopped as a warning bell rang in her mind. Don't do it, an inner voice warned. Why not? she wondered, and answered herself sadly, Because you *could* become an object of compassion—if he's being honest and you aren't one already...

She took a deep breath and sat down again. 'Sorry. I do believe you, and I...' she gestured '...was just feeling a little melodramatic I suppose. I'm better now. Thanks for—all this, but w-wouldn't it be b-better for both of us if I gave up your house?'

He stared at her intently then sat down opposite her. 'How would it affect your job?'

She winced inwardly, and not because of her job. 'Oh, I doubt it would really,' she said, and again not because it was true. 'We—er—seem to be pretty busy. Shall I see what I can do?'

'If there's the slightest difficulty I—why don't I tell them I've changed my mind about getting it done at all or I think it's too expensive? They couldn't blame you for that, could they?' he said slowly.

'Then get someone else? No.' She wasn't sure why she said it; it seemed to be mixed up with a sense of pride and a sense of chagrin. If he couldn't love her then she needed no favours from him... 'I'll find a way; I'd rather.'

He started to say something but her intercom from the front door of the building buzzed aggressively. He got up to answer it and told the taxi driver he'd be down in a few minutes.

'So that's it,' Juanita said tonelessly.

'Would you rather I'd told you this after we'd—made love?'

The silence was deafening.

'Would you rather,' he said with a sort of grim gentleness as if it was hurting him to say it, 'I'd allowed us to rush headlong like a runaway train into a relationship after knowing each other for such a short time, and really knowing so little about each other?' He stood before her and she had to tilt her head to look up at him. He'd never seemed taller but she couldn't doubt the bleak honesty in his eyes or the inescapable logic of what he'd said and how it echoed what she'd told herself so often. 'Don't you think,' he said, 'I've made enough mistakes as it is?'

She sighed—only a breath of sound, and when he put out his hand she took it and stood up herself.

But he let her hand go immediately and didn't try to touch her. 'Remember,' he said very quietly, 'you're brave and you're beautiful. And, though for the wrong reasons, your instincts about me were right all along. I'm sorry.' And then he touched her cheek fleetingly— and was gone.

'You look different, darling,' her mother said critically the next day. 'You look both haunted and beautiful and alive all at the same time. I could paint you——'

'No, thanks—I mean, I wouldn't have the patience for it.'

Her mother raised a thoughtful eyebrow but changed the subject. 'Did you ever get in touch with Damien? He is in Adelaide——'

'Yes, I did,' Juanita said briefly. 'Mum—do you think I—hide behind my walking stick?'

Her mother narrowed her beautiful eyes. 'I would hesitate to say so, darling, you've achieved absolute wonders but...funnily enough I bumped into your specialist the other day and we had quite a chat. Naturally he asked after you and, well, he did express the opinion that you might have given up the physiotherapy too soon.'

Juanita grimaced. 'It felt like years—it was.'

'I know. And I know I badgered you about it a lot until I could see it was making you more determined than ever——'

Juanita looked at her with unusual affection. 'Sorry. So you did.'

'Does your hip still pain you a lot?'

'Not a lot, but *yes*, it does sometimes and it can't seem to take a lot of pressure so...but that's a different thing from hiding behind a stick, wouldn't you say?'

Her mother looked at her even more intently. 'Has someone accused you of this?'

Juanita nodded reluctantly.

'The same man who's made you look—like this?'

Juanita thought of dissembling and she winced inwardly at her mother's automatic assumption, but of course it was true. 'He did suggest it might be more in my mind now.'

'And what right does he have to suggest things like that?'

Juanita smiled at her mother's haughty expression. 'All the same I haven't been able to help wondering if

I gave up too easily and whether it was because ... it was something to hide behind.'

'For the other reasons?' her mother queried quietly and with acute perception. 'My dear, that opinion was a voicing of, as they say these days, the worst case scenario. It was *not* cause to give up hope entirely. There are new techniques——'

'Perhaps. Or perhaps they were trying to let me down lightly. Mum...' Juanita hesitated '...how would you handle it? Would you tell a man before you began...anything with him or...?I mean obviously if you did plan to marry someone you would have to tell them that the likelihood of your having a baby was virtually nil, wouldn't you? But...'

Her mother stared at her. 'Who——?'

'I'm not planning to marry anyone, Mum, I'm just theorising.'

Her mother, Juanita thought, suddenly looked old and anxious, then she said intensely, 'To someone who loved you it shouldn't make one whit of difference. So if this man is more interested in populating the world in his image than you——'

'He's not—although it seems a shame. He's very good with kids.'

'I don't understand!'

Juanita grimaced. 'Forget I mentioned it. Can I see what you're working on now?'

She had an interview with her boss at Bluemoon the next day which was a lot more unequivocal than her discussion with her mother.

Her boss at Bluemoon, who was a part-owner of the company, was a man she respected for his vision, expertise and business sense, but he was also a plain speaker.

'What the hell's going on?' he demanded with a frown. 'I must warn you I don't take too kindly to losing accounts, Juanita, particularly not when I've made something of an exception and given you your own assignment earlier on in your career than I normally would have.'

'You won't lose it,' she said.

'I can't imagine how you can be so sure of that, but even if it were true, who the devil am I going to give it to? We're all flat-out. And the other reason I gave you the Walker account is because we have no one at the moment with the kind of vision you seem to have regarding old country houses.'

'I appreciate all that——'

'I hope you do, my dear. Perhaps it wouldn't be untimely to say that flair, which you undoubtedly have, is only half the battle in this game. What has upset you about this job?'

She hesitated.

'Is it too big for you?'

'No,' she said slowly, caught in a cleft stick. 'I mean, it is a big job but there are no structural changes required, the proportions of the house are wonderful and he doesn't want them changed, and it's all in good repair apart from the bathrooms. They're going to be the biggest job because they all need new fittings but the plumbing seems to be pretty straightforward and I've got advice on it anyway——' She stopped and bit her lip.

'He?' Her boss cocked an irate and intuitive eyebrow at her. 'Are you telling me Gareth Walker has made a pass at you? Look, if *that's* the problem and you haven't the experience to handle it, we may both well be wasting our time.'

She set her teeth and knew she was handling things incredibly badly. But other than the truth, which she was not prepared to go into, what to say? In any case, what difference would the truth make? she reflected suddenly. This was the hard-headed world of business and if she wanted to succeed she would have to learn to bury her emotions. She thought briefly of Gareth's suggestion but that too would have pitfalls that he mightn't realise. Once word got around that he'd engaged another company—and it would—she would still be perceived as having lost the account. And what else do I have but my career? she asked herself.

She said uncertainly, 'Perhaps I'm suffering from a lack of confidence.'

Her boss looked fractionally less irate. 'Bring me your presentation. We'll go through it together and I'll tell you what I think.'

An hour later he said, 'Juanita, this is bloody good. So gather your confidence, my dear, and go out and slay the world, not to mention Gareth Walker. Once people see your work they'll be queueing up for you.'

But how to go back? And would he want her back?

'I know you must be wondering why I'm here,' she said two days later, in his study. It was a bleak, wet afternoon and Wendy had let her in, with evident pleasure and no surprise. It would appear Gareth had not yet passed on the news.

'Sit down.' He ran a hand wearily through his hair. He looked disillusioned, she thought, as well as tired, and it hurt her to see the lines beside his mouth... Stop it, she warned herself. You can do it.

'I was wrong about being able to get someone else for you; we just don't appear to have anyone at the moment and——' she swallowed '—I was given to understand I would be...most unpopular if I didn't complete this job.'

'I see.' He picked up a pen, studied it for a moment then looked at her. She was wearing a pair of almond trousers and a corn-coloured cotton shirt. There were still raindrops netted in her hair, which was tied back as usual. 'What about my suggestion?'

She tried to explain. 'It's a very cut-throat business and everybody generally knows who's got what account,' she finished.

He grimaced. 'That didn't occur to me.'

'I know.'

There were a few moments' silence. 'Well, there's an alternative,' he said at last. 'It really doesn't matter if I put it off—another six months or whatever isn't going to make much difference.'

She couldn't help the hurt she felt—But I've just got to learn to deal with it, haven't I? she thought. And I've got to make myself believe there is no hope!

'No,' she said surprisingly steadily, then gestured. 'I mean, of course it's up to you. If you'd rather not ... see me again, I'd quite understand, but if I could do this job I'd feel ... This is a bit hard to explain but——' she looked down '—my professionalism is on the line in a way and it's very important to me. So... But please don't think I have any ideas of persuading you to change your mind about other things.' She closed her eyes briefly then made herself look up. 'I would also stay in Mittagong when I'm down, but at no cost to you, of course.'

'You think that would solve any problems we might have regarding ''other things'' quote unquote?' he queried quietly.

She bit her lip and rubbed her brow. 'Y-y-yes.'

He sat up and dropped the pen. 'No——'

She flinched visibly but said, 'All right, I understand——'

'I don't think you do. But I do understand what you've been trying to tell me and I understand about your career, so if you're prepared to give it a go I can only do the same. But you don't have to spend your own money to stay in Mittagong.'

'I'd rather, though——'

'Juanita,' he said evenly, 'this isn't going to be easy for either of us even if you'd be popping in from the moon, but if we're going to do it we might as well do it properly.'

She took a shaky breath. 'But do you *really* understand?'

'Yes.' His expression changed. 'We might even find it cures us. God knows,' he said drily, 'if it doesn't come home to you how difficult it is to live with someone like me...' He shrugged.

'It's still not going well?' Juanita ventured.

'No.'

'Oh. Well, I've brought down the presentation.' She bent down and pulled a glossy folder from her document case. 'Would you like to see it now?'

'I might as well.'

'The contract is there too.'

'Good.'

It took him about twenty minutes to go through the presentation with its sketches of every room, its attached samples, and he queried a few things but for the most part concentrated in silence, and Juanita stared out of the window at the rain.

Then he looked up at last. 'That's fine. It's more than fine actually. You have a lot of talent, Juanita.' And he picked up his pen.

'Before you sign that,' she said quickly, 'we always like to remind clients that of course some changes can be made if you find yourself absolutely hating something, but in the case of carpets and so it can be costly.'

He raised an eyebrow at her. 'I can imagine, but that's why I'm paying for your expertise—because I don't have the time or inclination to spend hours agonising over these things; and you don't need to worry—I won't carry on like some bored housewife who can't choose between pink and blue for the toilet-seat covers.' He signed the contract, drew up a cheque and handed them to her.

Gareth Walker just being Gareth Walker or was that a calculated way of saying it was only business between them now? she wondered. She said formally, 'Thank you. I . . . I'll do it as quickly as I can.'

'Well——' he stood up '—I hadn't got round to telling them you wouldn't be coming back—just in case anything like this happened—so I'm sure your old room is ready and waiting for you.'

She took a breath. 'That's great. I'll also try not to disturb you too much. You're lucky you have this retreat.'

'Am I?' He looked around broodingly. 'It's getting more and more like a prison.'

'Something will come up,' she said with a bright, reassuring smile although she felt as if her heart was breaking. 'That's what my mother says—when you least expect it some form of inspiration turns up.'

Which were to prove famous last words—at least, something turned up the very next day.

She went into Mittagong once again the next morning to consort with tradespeople and to make definite arrangements, and it was after lunch when she drove back. It had stopped raining overnight and was bright and sunny although the ground was still steaming—and there was a bright yellow sports car parked beside the fountain.

That its owner should be Laura Hennessey never entered her wildest imagination but that was undoubtedly who happened to stroll round the corner of the house with Gareth as Juanita alighted from her car. And it was Westminster, accompanying them, who gave vent to the first greeting in the form of a delighted bark of recognition and a surging up to her that made her stumble, lose her footing and sit heavily on the ground while he proceeded to lick her enthusiastically.

The next few minutes were confused but finally Westminster was consigned back to the stable area in disgrace, in Wendy's care. Juanita, now muddied and pale, was helped into the house by Gareth, and Laura Hennessey followed suit with a light-hearted remark that the dog was really only a puppy still—he apparently struck no fear into her heart at all, Juanita thought darkly as she tried to stop shaking.

'Are you all right?' Gareth asked as he guided her to a chair in the hall.

'Yes. Fine,' she said, but shakenly and feeling foolish.

He bent down in front of her and took her hands. 'It could have been worse——'

'I know. It could have been the fountain—sorry, it was really my fault; I panicked.'

'Sure? Not just being brave?'

She shook her head. 'Positive.'

'Good girl.' His eyes glinted with something like admiration then became tinged with amusement as he straightened. 'Well, I don't suppose I have to introduce you, do I? Laura, this is Juanita Spencer-Hill, an admirer of yours.'

Laura Hennessey was as slim but taller than she appeared on television, yet as perfectly groomed and vitally attractive with her cropped blonde hair, her expert make-up that highlighted a pair of rather exceptional yellowy hazel eyes, and her outfit, perfect for a day in the country, of a silk blouse tucked into beautifully cut jeans and brown brogues. All of which made Juanita glance down at her bedraggled self ruefully. This morning it had seemed like a good idea to wear a very pale primrose dress with a full skirt—it now seemed like the worst idea in the world. Added to that she'd grazed a wrist and it had bled on to her skirt and her hair was coming adrift, she discovered as she put a hand to it, from the silver clasp she wore.

'How do you do, Juanita?' Laura murmured, her gaze following almost exactly the path that Juanita's own had, and missing none of the dishevelment. 'I always feel so sorry for people who are afraid of dogs, don't you, Gareth?' she added. 'What they *don't* realise is they bring it on themselves. Once a dog senses you——'

'Westminster is a pretty overpowering kind of dog,' Gareth broke in easily. 'Nor is he as well-trained as I had hoped he was, but he actually likes Juanita.' He gestured wryly. 'What we need, I think, is a cup of tea; it certainly feels like teatime. Would you care to join us in the kitchen, Laura? A lot of the business of this house is conducted in the kitchen.' He smiled gravely.

'I thought you introduced me to your housekeeper?' Laura raised a thin, well-groomed eyebrow at him.

'She's actually filling in for her mother. And she will at this moment——' Gareth consulted his watch '—be setting out to pick up her twin brother and sister from school. Which is a relief to all and sundry—the fact that the terrible twins are back at school.'

Juanita glanced at the other girl, wondering what she would make of this. There was no doubting Laura's vigorous intelligence even if you hadn't seen her engaged in deadly debate, but what was also suddenly obvious was that everything to do with this house appeared to

be of deep, forthright interest to her—why? Juanita
wondered a bit dazedly. Why is she here at all for that
matter? Doesn't she realise what a fool he made of her?
And why do I feel as if I might not exist?

'Curiouser and curiouser!' Laura said gaily. 'I'd love
to have tea in the kitchen. You can tell me more at the
same time.' And she actually linked her arm through
Gareth's and waited for him to lead the way.

But Gareth unlinked himself politely and held out a
hand to Juanita. 'Would you like to freshen up first?'

'Th-thanks. Y-yes I would,' she stammered and braced
herself to stand up. 'No, please,' she added as he stared
down at her interrogatively, 'I am fine; I *don't* need help.'

He frowned then stepped back and murmured, 'Right.
We'll expect you shortly.'

'Oh——'

'I thought you'd be interested actually, Juanita,' he
overrode her. 'Laura has turned up with an idea of
making some sort of television special on modern literature that she'd like me to participate in.' He smiled,
a cool, chiselled movement of his lips yet there was a
glint in his eye as if the thought of it intrigued him. 'Do
join us.'

Tea was made and poured when Juanita joined them
in the kitchen, washed and brushed and changed into
her emerald tracksuit bottoms and white T-shirt.

And Laura was immediately gracious. 'Gareth's been
telling me about you, Juanita. What a wonderful house
to have *carte blanche* with! By the way, I've interviewed
your mother, your father *and* your brother. What a
family!' she marvelled.

'Thank you...' It was all Juanita could think of to
say.

Laura turned back to Gareth. 'Well, what's it to be?'

He appeared to meditate then he looked across at her, a very direct blue glance but curiously enigmatic. 'No,' he said quite gently.

Laura didn't even flinch. She said softly instead, 'That's not very sporting. Don't you think I deserve an opportunity to—even things up?'

'I don't—forgive me—I don't see how you could.'

There was a moment's silence but to Juanita it was particularly significant because it was almost tangible, the current that was flowing between these two intelligent, articulate and attractive people, and it was also bound up with their being of the opposite sex; it was part of it. And as she watched from the sideline, so to speak, she experienced a sense of disillusionment, then a sense of inadequacy and anger with herself that she'd ever let herself hope she could match Gareth Walker as this woman might...

'You'll never know until you try it,' Laura said, quite soberly. 'Nor do I give up easily,' she added. 'And for what it's worth, since I've given it more thought, your writing rather intrigues me. When you get tired of writing genre thrillers, why don't you try your hand at something with more depth? I'm quite sure the potential is there.'

Was that a stroke of genius? Juanita wondered as she lowered her lashes almost in pain for Gareth.

But he didn't take long to reply. He said, with not the least sign of resentment or anger, 'Oh, I don't know, Laura. I think it's a wise man who knows his limitations.'

She shrugged. 'But perhaps less wise to be afraid of trying to test one's limitations.' And the glance they exchanged was long and challenging until Laura smiled and added lightly, 'By the way, I'm staying with friends about a mile or two from here—did I mention it? No, well, I've got a whole week with them during which I'm going to relax, ride their admirable horses if the mood takes me—we could see more of each other...'

She left not long afterwards.

Wendy hadn't returned so Juanita washed up the tea things and thus was still in the kitchen when Gareth came back—via the back door, which he slammed the bottom half of shut. Then he cast himself down in a kitchen chair and said sardonically, 'What do you make of that?'

Juanita dried a cup carefully. 'I don't think I should make anything of it,' she said at last.

'Why the hell not? If you can dry the dishes in my house, surely you can venture an opinion. Do you think I'm going to leap on you every time we carry on a civilised conversation?'

'Civilised?' She looked at him ruefully, understanding his anger and frustration but not altogether seeing why it should be taken out on her. 'All right. I think it's quite plain. You got her in despite making her look a fool. So she wants a chance not only to avenge herself—er—intellectually, but also to see more of you.' She put the cup away and reached for another.

'"Got her in",' he echoed savagely. 'If you mean what I think you mean by that, you're wrong.'

Juanita glanced at him. He had his jeans-clad legs sprawled out, his arms folded across his old khaki shirt, and she felt her heart bump once or twice and wondered if he really was blind about the effect he had on most women.

'OK, I'm wrong,' she said with a shrug. 'Tell me what you think.'

'If I knew that I wouldn't be asking you,' he growled and shoved his hair off his forehead. 'But I do know the bloody woman riles the life out of me and I'm not the kind of person who usually gets riled this way!'

'I believe you,' Juanita murmured. 'Could it be because she and your writer's block are all bound up together at the moment? We more or less decided that once before.'

'We did, you're right,' he said grimly. 'But why her? I've come across *plenty* of literary purists in my time.'

Juanita was silent as she wiped the sink and hung up a tea-towel. Silent because, although he couldn't see it, or wouldn't, she could. And I've got the feeling anything he may have felt for me will pale beside what could be between them one day...

He said suddenly in a different, drier voice, making her start slightly and turn to him, 'How many women do you think I can be attracted to at the one time?'

'Gareth——'

'You don't want to go into it? It's what you're thinking, though, and it is my reputation at stake.' His blue eyes were sardonic.

She hesitated. 'It would not be unusual or unknown— at least two, perhaps.'

'At least? Why not make it three or four?'

'Stop it,' she whispered. 'We made a bargain—at least I agreed to what *you* said, and I'm only here because . . .' Her mouth worked.

'Then perhaps you shouldn't dry up any more dishes while you're here.'

'This has to be *so* illogical!' They stared at each other and, notwithstanding all else, his gaze as it roamed over her was curiously intimate despite the hostility also in his eyes. And it turned her own hostility into something else. She felt as taut as a bow-string but achingly aware of him. She felt, and it amazed her, like slapping his face but ending up in his arms. She felt like making love to him, but coolly and always in control until he was helpless with desire—she experienced a range of emotions and wasn't at all sure whether they were love or rage, but was certain there was only one satisfactory solution to them. She wanted, with an almost savage intensity, to go to bed with him...

She closed her eyes, swallowed several times and tried to bring her wayward body under control, to remove the almost physical sensation of his skin on hers, his hands on her, her lips on his....

The kitchen door flew open and Steven raced in. 'Gareth, Gareth—Wendy's hurt herself, she can't get out of the car!'

What Wendy had done was get out of the car to open the gate—something Steven and Rebecca normally took turns to do, but because there was still a lot of mud about and because she was already muddy she'd decided to do it herself—only to slip and fall awkwardly and at least sprain, if not break, her ankle.

'I can't believe it,' she said palely as Gareth carried her into the kitchen. 'Look at it—it only happened a few minutes ago!'

'Mmm.' He removed her shoe and gently prodded the swollen flesh. Wendy winced. 'OK. What we need to do is get an ice pack on to it—and give Dr Smith a call.'

A severe sprain was Dr Smith's pronouncement, which required several days off it.

'But I can't!' Wendy protested.

'Yes, you can,' Gareth said wryly. 'Look, you can't even put it on the floor, let alone stand on it. Don't worry, kiddo! We can cope.'

'How?'

'I'm not as useless as I look,' he replied. 'And it's off to bed with you and no arguments,' he added firmly.

Juanita helped Wendy to change and get into bed. 'It was going so well too,' Wendy said disconsolately. 'I really don't know how on earth he's going to cope, what with his book and so on.'

'I . . . I'll help,' Juanita heard herself say.

Wendy was transformed. 'Would you?'

'Well, if he wants me to.'

'Why wouldn't he—if *you* don't mind?'

Juanita didn't reply to this.

They met in the passage that linked the domestic quarters to the house. 'All right?' He cocked an eyebrow at her.

'Yes. But worried. I . . . offered to help.'

'Did you, now?'

'Yes,' Juanita said with some grimness. 'Despite your aversion to my washing up, don't you think in the circumstances it's the sensible thing to do? At least I can do the cooking and wash a few clothes—the house is going to be in a mess anyway shortly.'

'My aversion to your washing up was not——'

'Let's not go into all that again,' she said angrily. 'I—— '

'All right, but let's get one thing straight.' He looked at her assessingly. 'If you haven't forwarded that contract and cheque yet we can tear them up and—take the other option I postulated. If this is going to be too hard for you, in other words.'

Despite the drama of Wendy's accident, Juanita's mind was still reeling from the impact of what had happened to her earlier. Yet it only made her more determined, she found, and angrier. 'I can cope,' she said tautly. 'I'm not so sure about you, though. So *you* tell me what you want to do. If you like, I can be out of here in about ten minutes.'

He narrowed his eyes. Then he said softly, 'By all means stay, Juanita. I'm not a hundred per cent sure what we're doing battle about at the moment but if

you're sure you want to fight on, why not? And——'
he smiled faintly ' —right at this moment I could do with
some help.'

She clenched her teeth then said briskly. 'Good. I'll
have dinner ready in an hour.' And she walked past him
towards the kitchen. But it was a long time before her
mental sinews, as well as some of her muscles, un-
clenched themselves, and then she had to wonder tiredly
if she wasn't, like Xanthe, as mad as a March hare.

CHAPTER EIGHT

THINGS went surprisingly well for a day and a half. But then again she only saw Gareth at mealtimes for any length of time and the presence of Rebecca and Steven helped considerably. They were not there to help her when Gareth came swearing into the kitchen at about two o'clock in the afternoon, because someone was banging beneath his study window.

Juanita was sitting at the table surrounded by papers. 'Oh, it's the plumber,' she said. 'He's moving——'

'I don't care what he's doing, he'll just have to stop,' he blazed. 'Anyway, why was I not informed he was to be here today? What the hell do *you* know about plumbing? I could end up with crossed drains and God knows what! Who *is* supervising him?'

'I am.' Juanita took a deep breath. 'But for that matter Rebecca or Steven could be. It's a very simple job, believe me.'

'You may think it is, although I still doubt your expertise in these matters, and for future reference don't start *anything* like this again without consulting me.' He glared at her, his eyes bluer than ever, his hair all awry as if he'd been raking his hand through it.

'Consulting you!' Juanita said bitterly. 'You *told* me you didn't have the time to agonise over the details of it, or words to that effect, so I assumed——'

'Well, you were wrong,' he said curtly. 'I may not have the time or inclination to go into the minutiae of it, but don't imagine——' his eyes glinted sardonically '——that I can sit by while people tear up and bash away at my house without wondering what the bloody hell they're doing!'

'They're *not* tearing anything up or bashing anything down. He's merely moving a couple of pipes today in a guest bathroom that no one uses and for the rest of it he'll be installing the more modern bathroom equipment.'

'I still want to know what's going on and when it's going on,' he said through his teeth.

'Right,' she returned dangerously, 'I'll post notices on your study door in future. But why don't you have a chat to him if you're so concerned? Or are you not capable of a simple common courtesy like that?'

'Don't get too clever with me, Juanita,' he warned.

'Clever!' she retorted. 'That's not being clever. You're just being impossible—and it's time you were going to pick up the twins anyway.'

He said something beneath his breath, there was a tentative knock on the back door and the plumber peered in. 'Er—anyone home?'

The change that came over Gareth Walker incensed Juanita all the more. He introduced himself blandly, apologised for what must have sounded suspiciously like a domestic row in progress and expressed an interest in seeing what was going on.

'Happy to show you,' the plumber replied. 'Always feel more comfortable dealing with a bloke—that is——'

'Don't bother to explain,' Juanita rasped. 'I hate the whole lot of you if you must know!'

Gareth ushered him out with a grin. 'That's done it, mate.' He closed the bottom half of the door carefully.

Juanita took some very deep breaths and restrained herself from throwing things.

And it was an effort, when they met again over dinner, to be barely polite to him although no one appeared to notice, helped by the fact that Wendy was allowed up on crutches so she supervised the twins' homework after the meal. Juanita spent some more time on the paperwork and the always tricky business of working painters and plasterers, wallpaper-hangers, carpet-layers, carpenters and tilers in with each other. And she worked on after Wendy and the twins had gone to bed, then pushed everything away suddenly and dropped her head into her hands.

How could I not have known, she wondered, what it would be like? How can you be so angry with someone yet—hunger for them like this?

'If it's any consolation, I feel as guilty as hell.'

Juanita lifted her head slowly. He was standing in the doorway, his hands shoved into his pockets, and as their eyes locked she read tiredness and something she couldn't quite name in his. Not tenderness or affection—a rather dark disaffection if anything, yet she got the strangest feeling that it wasn't directed at her but at himself.

She shrugged, a slight movement of her shoulders.

'Particularly in light of how you've helped,' he added. 'You must think I'm—a boor and a bully.'

For some reason this brought a slight smile to her lips. And she said, 'I should be used to it, shouldn't I?'

He came over at last and sat down opposite her. 'The artistic temperament? That makes me feel no less—guilty.'

'That will pass too,' she murmured, and gathered her papers.

'I wonder. Why are you working so late?' he queried without giving her a chance to comment.

'I was trying to work out a way to speed things up but it's such a juggling act as it is...' She gestured.

He was silent for a time then he said, 'Tell me something else——' His gaze roamed over her, taking in the simple white blouse she wore with a flared blue cotton skirt, the way her hair was coming adrift. 'Is it my imagination or are you using your stick far less than you used to?'

She bit her lip. 'No. I mean, it's not your imagination.'

'Why?'

She glanced at him briefly. 'I took your advice.'

'How so?'

She fiddled with her papers. 'I...well, it occurred to me...' She started again. 'I got so tired of it all I g-gave up the physiotherapy sooner than I should have. At least, I went back to the specialist and he was of the opinion that my hip will still respond to physio, and exercise. So that's what I'm doing, and trying to rely less on my stick. But it could still take time.'

'I'm proud of you.'

She looked at him fully. 'Thanks.'

'Your stammer seems better too.'

'That could have something to do with——'

'Being angry a lot of the time?'

She grimaced. 'You did tell me it improved my fluency.'

'You know,' he said very quietly, 'you could look back on all this one day and—put it down to experience.'

Juanita stood up abruptly because she was suddenly dangerously close to tears. 'Could I? I'm tempted to think it will always be like a nightmare but be that as it may—I'm going to bed.'

He didn't attempt to stop her.

He was also not in evidence at all the next morning.

'Where could he be?' Juanita asked Wendy with a frown. 'It's almost time to drive the kids to school.'

'Did you ring the stables?'

She nodded. 'He hasn't been seen down there—I can drive Rebecca and Steven but it just seems strange.'

Wendy narrowed her eyes. 'Have you actually gone into his study?'

'No, but I knocked.'

Wendy looked relieved. 'Go in and check—I'm pretty sure that's where he'll be. Sometimes he writes nearly all night then falls asleep on the settee.'

He was, sprawled out in his clothes, his head on his arms, looking impossibly uncomfortable but obviously deeply asleep. He didn't stir as she opened the door and tiptoed in. But it was also a scene of chaos that met her startled gaze. There was a snow-drift of crumpled-up papers on the floor, as if he'd printed out a chapter or two on his word processor and hated every word, even to the extent of balling up each page individually and hurling them around the room.

She glanced at him again but she couldn't see his face, only the rumpled dark fairness of his hair falling over his arm, but it was as if someone had squeezed her heart and where there had been anger there was now compassion...

She was quiet on the drive to school—not that Steven and Rebecca noticed. They chattered non-stop about the long weekend coming up the weekend after next and whether Wendy's ankle would be recovered enough for them to spend it in Sydney with a friend of their mother's so they could visit her as much as possible over the three days as had been planned for a while.

'I'm sure it will by then,' Juanita said absently when consulted.

'Will you stay and look after Gareth?' Steven queried, bringing Juanita out of her reverie somewhat. 'He sure needs someone to look after him at the moment,' he continued.

'I...well, we'll see,' Juanita temporised, and was saved by the fact that they arrived at the school.

So she had two things on her mind for the rest of the day but, for reasons buried in her subconscious probably, one loomed larger than the other. She had in fact bought one of his books when she'd returned to Sydney and, despite herself, enjoyed it thoroughly. He might be no Graham Greene but he was able to paint an interesting portrait of the country he wrote about and the twists and turns in the plot had held her riveted. What she'd appreciated even more, though, was his characterisation—he'd made a small arms-dealer and his mistress, a cellist full of deep and brooding passion who occasionally carried weapons of destruction in her cello case for him, fully believable and sometimes hilarious. But it was his hero she kept thinking about during that day. A man torn between the philosophy of the political end justifying the means but the brutality of those means.

And finally, after seeing little of him during the day, she bearded him in his study late in the afternoon.

He looked up and his eyes narrowed as she hesitated in the doorway. 'A problem?' he queried.

'No. Well, y-yes but not mine. May I come in?'

'Of course, but I hope it's not to tell me the plumber has——'

'Nothing like that,' she said hastily. 'That's all going really well.'

He smiled faintly. 'Good. Would you like to sit down or is this just a passing visit?'

'I'll sit down,' she said, but hesitated again and wondered whether she was mad. All the paper had been disposed of, she saw.

'You're in two minds,' he murmured, his eyes suddenly intent. 'Does that mean whatever you've come to tell me is—momentous or disastrous despite not being anything to do with the plumbing?'

'No, it means I don't know—you might th-think it's ridiculous.' She bit her lip.

'I won't know until you try me,' he pointed out. 'Sit down and have a go.'

'It's about your book,' she blurted out, and sat down hurriedly.

He raised his eyebrows and there was genuine surprise in his eyes as well as something else she couldn't put a name to. Then he frowned. 'Go on.'

'I have now read one of your books,' she said stiffly.

'That also surprises me,' he drawled.

'Yes, well, I enjoyed it,' she returned somewhat militantly and added before he could take issue, 'And it struck me that in this one——' she told him which one she'd read '—your main character was grappling with a real dilemma.'

'So he was.'

'As you are,' she said quietly.

'In regard to you?'

Juanita blinked. 'Oh, no!' she said hastily. 'I didn't mean that—in any case I don't think you are...'

He smiled with no amusement. 'I can assure you I am.'

Juanita started to feel hot. 'But it was you...' she whispered, then couldn't go on.

'So it was,' he said drily. 'That doesn't mean to say that the mere act of putting an end to it has stopped my thoughts or—other things.'

She couldn't tear her eyes away from his although there was nothing in them that was particularly intimate. 'Are you saying——? I suppose it is my fault if that's true,' she said huskily, and tried to say something more but nothing coherent would come so she closed her mouth and looked away defeatedly.

He sat forward. 'I'm sorry. I didn't mean to produce that effect—shall we get back to my book?'

She put a hand to her mouth as if to still that insidious and treacherous stammer. 'I wondered,' she said after a long moment, 'if you could put your own dilemma about popular literature and the capital L kind—er—into a story somehow. P-perhaps a character suffering something s-similar? I just wondered whether writing about it mightn't bring it back into perspective for you or add other perspectives, or simply...get it off your chest.' She pressed her hands together, still not looking at him.

The silence seemed to run on and on until she could have died of embarrassment and was finally forced to look at him—— To find him staring straight at her, but not as if he was seeing her at all, and her instinct was to slip away; indeed she made an awkward move but his gaze refocused and he said slowly, 'Why on earth didn't I think of that? I've got this bloke sucked into a counter-espionage racket quite accidental—if I made him a writer going through what I'm going through and going mad not only because of it but because of what's happening to him otherwise...'

Juanita relaxed. 'Not,' she said, uncertainly, though, 'that it's a moral dilemma as was in your other book——'

'It doesn't matter. I don't always go for moral dilemmas but I do like them not to be straight-up-and-down blokes. I wonder, though——' he looked at her, with a frown in his eyes '—whether...' But he didn't finish his sentence.

'Wonder?' Juanita said at last.

'Nothing.' He seemed to wrench his thoughts back to her. 'I was—just thinking.'

'Well, I'll leave you to it.' She stood up and smiled sketchily.

'Juanita...'

She stopped at the door and looked back to see him staring at her as if in two minds. But in the end, he only said quietly, 'Thank you.'

'My pleasure,' she murmured, and had to tear her gaze away.

Three days later, when the house was in a mild state of uproar with the painter making his preparations, a carpet firm taking measurements and a tiler working on the bathrooms, Laura Hennessey rode up on a large, spirited chestnut.

Juanita winced as she glanced out of the drawing-room window and realised who it was. Gareth had been working as if possessed and apparently oblivious to all noise and disruption. In fact she got the feeling that the house could have fallen down around him, which made her smile to remember their run-in over the plumber. He rarely even appeared for meals, and between them she and Wendy tried to concoct appetising offerings which they delivered on trays. His one form of exercise was a ride early morning and evenings. The net result of all this was that the household was peaceful although the house itself was in a mess.

'Amazing,' Wendy, who was almost fully mobile now, said once with a shake of her ponytail. 'Men are quite strange, aren't they?'

'Indeed they are,' Juanita replied wryly.

'I mean, if you'd told me he could write through this when he makes such a fuss sometimes over the littlest things, I wouldn't have believed you.'

'Let's just hope it lasts...'

'Ah, Juanita!' Laura said as she slid off the horse and tied it to a veranda post. 'Things are humming by the look of it.' She gestured to the mixture of vans parked about the fountain.

'They are,' Juanita agreed. 'I'm trying to get it done as quickly as possible.'

Laura smiled. It was a fresh, windy day and her cheeks glowed and she gave off the aura of sparkling health and vitality. 'Is the bard home?' she queried.

Juanita hesitated. 'He's writing,' she said slowly.

There was a sudden tense little pause as Laura narrowed her eyes upon Juanita then murmured, 'Why do I get the feeling I'm not very welcome? And—forgive me—but is it your place to decide who sees him and who doesn't?'

'Not at all,' Juanita responded, suddenly wishing violently that Wendy hadn't gone to town leaving her in this position. 'I——'

But Laura didn't let her finish. 'It crossed my mind the last time I was here that you—that there were certain—currents at work between you and Gareth.' She smiled faintly. 'Not that I blame you. The man's sheer dynamite, isn't he? But have you managed to stake any kind of claim, so to speak?'

'I have not,' Juanita said stiffly as the blood ran to her cheeks.

'Good!' Laura said blithely. 'Then you won't mind if I try to, will you?'

Juanita actually managed to smile although it left the muscles of her face feeling strained. 'No. He's in his study—would you like me to show you the way?'

*   *   *

'Don't spring uninvited guests upon me like that again, Juanita,' Gareth said coldly to her several hours later.

She looked at him across the kitchen table. They'd just finished dinner and Wendy had taken the twins to a school concert. It had not been a comfortable meal. 'I think you're labouring under a misapprehension. Two,' she said coolly. 'I'm not your housekeeper and secondly, it would have taken an army to keep her out.'

'But you could have told her *I* was out,' he said, still looking grim.

'You really are impossible, aren't you?' she grated through her teeth. 'Why should I tell lies on your behalf?'

'You know how I feel about the blasted woman; you obviously knew and appreciated what I was going through—in the name of human charity if nothing else, would one little white lie have been such an imposition?' He eyed her mockingly.

'Yes, it would have,' she retorted. 'As it was, I laid myself open to being suspected of—oh, this is ridiculous!' She stood up and began to clear the table.

'Suspected of?' he drawled.

'Nothing,' she flashed and banged the little silver condiment tray on to the sideboard so that the bottles rattled.

'As a matter of fact she told me what she suspected you of.'

Juanita froze then turned back to him incredulously. '*What* did she tell you?'

He smiled a slow, lazy smile but his eyes still managed to remain cool. 'She said, "You could have a problem with your interior decorator, dear Gareth. I think she's fallen in love with you".'

'Did she, now?' Juanita managed to speak perfectly calmly and plainly. 'Well, that might have been true once but, *dear* Gareth,' she mimicked, 'your interior decorator has come to her senses. And you *were* right. No one in their right senses could cope with you. I wonder if I shouldn't enlighten Laura about it all? Before she gets too serious about staking her claim with you—which is what she said to *me*.'

'Dear me,' he murmured, 'so *you* were right.'

'Of course I was right. The only blind person around here is *you*.'

'That doesn't mean to say I reciprocate those sentiments in any way.'

'You spent two hours with her,' Juanita pointed out. 'You could just be fighting it for the sake of a fight; I wouldn't put that past you at all. And who's to say she mightn't suit all your requirements? I would imagine her career is extremely important to her, I would imagine the last thing she would want to do is abandon it to sink into a sea of domesticity and maternity—you two could very well come up with some kind of arrangement that would be perfect for both your outsized egos.'

'I hesitate to say this, Juanita, but all that sounded rather bitchy,' he said quite gently and with a glint of sudden humour in his eyes.

She picked up the mustard pot and threw it at him. It missed and shattered on the table. He glanced at the shards of glass then pushed his chair back, stood up slowly and stepped towards her.

'Don't you dare!' she panted, aware suddenly of how tall and strong he looked and, curiously, becoming even angrier. 'What gives you the right to preach to *me*? You think you can treat me like the hired help, you . . . you tell me I mustn't fall in love with you but you keep bringing the subject up! Why was it necessary to tell me what Laura said? I must tell you—and I have *no* hesitation in saying this—it was because you're no different from those men who . . . Gareth?' she said uncertainly in quite a different voice.

'Mmm?' He didn't attempt to touch her although a bare foot separated them but there was something oddly heavy-lidded about his eyes as they rested on her flushed face, as if nothing she said or did was making much impression on him, and suddenly it frightened her.

'Wh-what are you going t-to do?'

'What would you like me to do?'

She bit her lip. 'N-nothing.'

He smiled absently and reached out at last to touch her face. 'So you believe I'm an unmitigated cad now? Perhaps I am but I have to tell you that there's a limit to what most men can stand, much as it might be an embarrassment to have to admit it. And the way you fit into this house, the way you fit into my life and even have the nerve to throw things at me when I'm impossible is testing things to that limit. So perhaps it's as well you have come to your senses, Juanita. Because if I'm tempted to overstep the limit, as I am right now, you'll be able to have the will-power for both of us, won't you?'

Her lips parted as she sorted through the implications of what he'd said and her eyes widened as she registered the subtle attack, the implicit mockery, the placing of the responsibility for this state of affairs squarely on her shoulders. And she could have cried at the unfairness and unkindness of it; she wanted to tell him it was all his fault because he wouldn't let her love him even though it was what they both wanted...

She closed her eyes and whispered, 'You told me once you weren't kind—now I believe you.'

'I also told you once this wasn't going to be easy,' he said very quietly. 'Perhaps you understand better now why it isn't.'

'If you think it's been easy for me; if that's what you're saying——' She broke off as she realised there were tears rolling down her cheeks, then suddenly didn't care. 'Why are you so sure you can't change? Why, if things are the way they are between us, can't you at least have some hope? I can't mean terribly much to you if I don't at least . . . bring you some hope.'

'On the contrary——' he took her chin in his hand and brushed the tears with his thumb '—it's the other way around. Believe it or not, the likes of Laura Hennessey are a dime a dozen these days. And I'm quite sure we could come to some satisfactory arrangement, were I so minded, that would leave neither of us devastated when the time came to move on to other things or people. But not so you, and a leopard doesn't change his spots, although, God knows, I wish I could.'

'What——' Juanita swallowed and licked her lips '—if I were to tell you that I could never tie you down, I could never re-create what happened in your marriage?'

He frowned and his hand stilled. 'What do you mean?'

She told him, haltingly.

'No,' he said disbelievingly and with sudden pain in his eyes.

'Yes,' she whispered.

They stared at each other and then suddenly she was in his arms and he was stroking her hair and saying her name over and over as she wept into his shoulder.

'I'm fine now,' she said, but shakily, some time later.

He'd picked her up and carried her into his study, closing the door and sitting down on the settee with her in his lap. And he'd rocked her as if she were a child until the storm of emotion had waned.

He said nothing but kept stroking her hair.

'I shouldn't have told you,' she said huskily against his shoulder and unwittingly fiddled with a button of his shirt. 'I suppose——' She stopped and thought for a moment, and uncovered a sense of truth in her heart. 'I couldn't stop *myself* hoping that there could be some sort of future for us, so that's why I did tell you. But now I'll never know, if there is, how much of it will be because you feel sorry for me.' She grimaced.

'And that's why you got so upset the day I accused you of mental sterility or words to that effect,' he said drily.

'Yes. But you weren't to know.'

'I should be shot all the same.'

'Oh, no.' A faint smile trembled on her lips.

'Have you... is this a constant cross that you bear, Juanita?'

She considered. 'If you mean do I, every time I see a baby, gnash my teeth and decline into despair, no,' she said slowly. 'Although it could come. I don't think I've got to the stage—I mean, even if I were normal I think I'm the kind of person who would come to that clucky, broody sort of state later than most. But I still feel sad when I see Rebecca and Steven——'

'It's not that you're abnormal,' he said.

'No. Not precisely.'

'I wish I could make you believe that.'

'You could,' she said wryly, then sat up with an urgent movement. 'I didn't mean that...'

'What did you mean?' he asked, turning her slightly with his hands on her waist so that she was facing him.

She lowered her lashes and felt her cheeks grow hot.

'Tell me, Juanita.'

She licked her lips and thought of trying to dissimulate but then she lifted her lashes and looked into his eyes, and knew that, whatever the cost, she could only be honest with Gareth Walker. 'I've often wondered whether the fact that I could bring some real joy to a man—I mean physically and mentally so that, even for a while, without each other we would only feel like a half a person—would compensate for the fact that I couldn't give him children. I've thought that if I could I might feel normal then. But I could be wrong, I might feel worse; who knows? And I suppose because you're the only man I've really...well, you probably know what I mean, plus the fact that you wouldn't want my children anyway, it seemed—I can't believe I'm saying this,' she whispered, feeling the heat flood up from the base of her throat again.

His eyes were more sombre than she'd seen them as he said, 'It's not that I wouldn't want your children——'

'Any children, then,' she amended. 'You must know what I mean——'

'Yes, I think I do,' he said after a long pause, and slowly ran his fingers from the nape of her neck through her hair, releasing what was left in its clasp. 'As a matter of fact a lot of things about you, without your even trying, are a joy to me. Your hair for one. I often long to take it out of its clasp; I'll always remember how you looked with a flower pinned into it. Then there's your mouth,' he said barely audibly and with that heavy-lidded look of earlier. 'I have the most urgent desire at times to crush those cool lips and make them flower for me. Like this.'

'Gareth,' she gasped as he bent his head, 'I wasn't...I was only trying to be *honest*, not——'

'I know.' His breath fanned her forehead. 'I'm only being honest too. Don't fight and don't panic; we've done this before, remember?' And his lips closed over hers.

'But I've never done this before,' she said, not with panic but a little uncertainty in her voice some time later.

'I know. It doesn't matter—to me, that is,' he said
softly, and she wondered how he'd guessed that any reservations she might have now were to do with disap-
pointing him. Because the truth of the matter was that
her poor body, which had yearned for him at times so
intensely over the past days, was responding to what he
was doing to her like a flower opening up to the sun.
And it was as if her soul too was being nourished, because Gareth Walker, at the same time as he made her
feel achingly alive, was making love to her mind... There
was no hurry as he not only caressed her out of her
clothes but caressed her psyche with what he said and
the way he touched her.

'You're so good at it, though,' she murmured and
linked her arms behind his head. 'I might not be.'

She felt him smile against her breast. 'If I am it's because you're—exquisite,' he said rather wryly, 'and if
you're not, it will be my fault.'

'But——'

'Hush,' he said and twined his fingers through her
hair. 'The only thing you need to tell me is if I'm hurting
you.'

'Oh, no,' she said softly. 'But surely I can do better
than that? Well——' she bit her lip '—do this anyway.'
And she ran her hands slowly and lingeringly down the
long, bare length of his back.

'Be my guest,' he murmured, his voice not quite as
steady, 'but I must warn you of the effect it's liable to
have on me.'

'Oh?' she said innocently, her lips curving and her
hands wandering at will now as she delighted in the feel
of all the lean, strong planes of his body.

'Mmm...' He shuddered slightly. 'This,' he added, gathering her into his arms and moulding her to him, 'my beautiful, talkative seductress.'

Her lips parted and her breathing came faster but she managed to say, 'That makes me feel...wonderful and more equal.'

He said her name on a laughing breath but from then on she said not a word because what was happening to her defied description.

And when they finally lay still in each other's arms, she was exhausted but filled with the kind of joy she'd never known, and speech seemed not only impossible but entirely unnecessary. She fell asleep like a child in his arms.

CHAPTER NINE

JUANITA woke only minutes before her bedroom door opened, and dazedly realised it must be quite late for several reasons. The early morning bird chorus was not in progress and the room was quite light despite the curtains being drawn, and she could hear someone hammering. Then other things impinged on her consciousness—the different state of her body, the fact that she was in her own bed, decorously clad in her own nightgown, although she didn't remember getting there, and she sat up suddenly with her hands to her cheeks and her heart pounding.

That was when the door opened and Gareth walked in bearing a tray. 'Ah. That was well timed,' he murmured. 'Good morning.' He set the tray down and came to sit on the side of the bed. He looked exactly as he always did, wearing one of his favourite old khaki shirts and jeans, but the sight of him—the little glint in his eye, the way his hair fell, his hands—increased her heart-rate even further.

'G-good m-morning,' she stammered then her eyes widened with anxiety. 'You can't do this!' she gasped. 'It was bad enough—how did I get here? Not that it matters, thank goodness I did, but——'

He took her hands and smiled faintly. 'I put you here after you fell asleep. I thought it was what you would prefer. I also told Wendy that you hadn't been feeling well and not to disturb you,' he said gravely.

'Oh.' She licked her lips. 'All the same...' She stopped and wished she'd had time to compose herself although she suddenly doubted it was possible.

'All the same?' he teased.

'I...Gareth—the children *and* Wendy—we can't——'

'Relax,' he said with a grimace. 'I'm of the same mind as it happens so they're not here.'

'Not *here*?'

'I've sent them up to Sydney to their mother's friend. It will give them a bit more than a week with Mrs Spicer instead of just the long weekend. I told them that, with the house the way it is, the fewer people here the better, which is probably true, and I reassured Wendy that at just seven Rebecca and Steven would not be educationally blighted for the rest of their lives by missing another week of school—also true, I'm sure. And I pointed out how much their mother must be missing them. I didn't have to do much more persuading at all, especially——' a wicked little glint lit his eyes now '—as *Steven* pointed out that, with you here to look after me, they had nothing to worry about.'

Some of the concern left Juanita's expression but some remained. 'What time is it?' she asked lamely.

His lips twisted. 'Ten or thereabouts. Of course it's a two-way thing,' he continued. 'We could look after each other, you might say.' And he calmly released her hands, drew back the bedclothes and lay down beside her.

She opened her mouth to protest but he stilled it by the simple expedient of taking her in his arms and kissing her deeply. Then he rearranged the pillows more comfortably and, still with an arm around her, said quite differently, 'Tell me something—did I do the right thing?'

Juanita remembered his lovemaking and the rapture that she had so willingly participated in and she trembled and laid her cheek against his shoulder with a little sigh. 'I don't know about right,' she said huskily, 'but it was…lovely. More so than I—dreamt it could be. I only hope it was the same for you.'

'It was.' He didn't smile and there was a genuine gravity in his voice.

She sat up and looked down at him as if by looking into his eyes she could see into his soul. 'What does that mean?' she whispered.

'Only that you're stunning and warm and wonderful. And it's going to be particularly hard to get up off this bed and give you breakfast but there's a gaggle of tradespeople tramping around the place all getting in each other's way, not to mention *mine*——'

She giggled. He looked injured. 'That amuses you?'

'Yes, it does,' she confessed, still smiling. 'I don't know why.'

'You're even more beautiful when you laugh,' he murmured, sitting up but taking her face in his hands. 'I hope——' He stopped.

Her smile faded but her eyes were calm as she kissed the inside of his wrist. 'Let's not think about it,' she said after a moment. 'Why don't we…? May I treat you to dinner tonight, Mr Walker? When all these tradespeople have left us in peace and we have the house to ourselves?'

His eyes were never bluer, she thought, although as unreadable too as they'd ever been. But he said simply, 'I'd love that. Thank you, Miss Spencer-Hill.'

It was six o'clock, however, before the last worker left and Juanita sat down at the kitchen table to get her breath. She had an old pair of jeans on and a white scarf bound round her hair, she had paint on her hands and a streak of it on her shirt, and she'd seen Gareth only once during the day when he'd brought her a sandwich and a cup of tea and insisted she eat it in the study with him—the only oasis of peace and quiet.

And she thought, as she sat, that it had been good for her to have such a busy day; it had even been deliberate because it had taken her mind off other things, although it had been impossible to forget what had happened to her the night before...

'Penny for 'em?' a voice said behind her.

She turned to see Gareth right behind her and eyeing her quizzically.

She grimaced and stood up. 'I haven't even started dinner,' she said ruefully, but he ignored this and took her in his arms.

'I've been dying to do this all day—you know, when I hired an interior decorator, I didn't expect her to actually buck in and do the work.' He touched her nose.

She squinted down. 'Paint?'

'Paint,' he agreed.

'I wasn't actually painting——'

'You could have fooled me.' He kissed the tip of her nose.

'I was *mixing* really—I wanted to get just the right colour.'

'Did you?'

'Yes.'

'And what were you doing when I saw you sandpapering an architrave?'

'Oh, that—well, I was just giving the carpenter a hand.'

He kissed her lips with a smile in his eyes. 'You look happy.'

She felt herself melt inside and doubted whether she'd ever been happier than just standing in the circle of his arms, breathing in the heady essence of him and, to her surprise, when she was tempted to kiss the strong column of his throat, she did just that, lightly, but it made him take her scarf off and stroke her hair and they rested together for a minute or more.

Then he said, 'I've got an idea. Instead of immediately slaving over a hot stove, why don't we have a swim and a drink?'

'I'd love that.'

And to be in his arms in the pool, although decorously clad in her costume, brought another dimension to the sheer sensuality her body was coming to know. And to know that she was arousing him equally.

'I think we ought to think about dinner,' she said, faintly pink-cheeked, after about half an hour in the pool.

'Do you indeed?' His hair was plastered to his head, his eyes glinting with that familiar devilry. 'Why is that?' He lifted her in his arms so that she was looking down at him with water streaming off her.

'One should eat,' she said after a long moment, her own eyes grave.

'We have all night.'

'One should really eat regular meals, however.'

'What about food for the soul?'

She touched her wet palm to his cheek and loved the faintly rough feel of it. 'If you mean what I think you mean . . . ?' He nodded. 'Well, that's important too, of course——'

'Of course. Unfortunately, I have to tell you that my soul is in much more urgent need of placating than my stomach.'

'Your soul?' she queried innocently. 'That's an unusual way of putting it.'

'It's all bound up together,' he assured her. 'Anyway, at this moment you are food for my soul as well as my body. I can't wait any longer,' he said simply.

*   *   *

'There's an old saying,' Juanita said dreamily as she lay naked on a double bed in a guest bedroom—one of the few rooms to escape any form of renovation as yet.

'There is?' Gareth ran his hand idly down her body. 'Tell me.'

She turned her head on the pillow and her lips quivered. 'It's to do with horses actually. They say you should never back a racehorse second time up—I mean at its second start.'

'I don't see the—is there a connection?'

She didn't say anything for a while, then, 'I couldn't help wondering if I imagined last night and, even if I hadn't, whether I could be the same again.'

'You can—trust me.' His hand moved back to her breasts and she shivered with delight as he plucked first one nipple then the other very gently.

And she kissed his shoulder and permitted herself the pleasure of touching his body in return and found she was fascinated by their differences—the soft paleness of her skin against his tan, how slender she felt against his strength, how big and strong his hands felt on her but how gentle. In fact she was so fascinated that she almost forgot to answer. 'Well, if you say so——' her lips curved '—I won't argue.'

'Good. Because——' he took her by surprise and gathered her into his arms and rolled her on top of him '—I wouldn't want to spoil our second time up by any sense of disagreement.'

Juanita blinked at him but he returned her regard seriously and said equally seriously, 'Comfortable?' He crossed his hands behind his head.

She moved softly on him as if testing it out. 'Uh-huh. Is there anything I should do?'

'You could keep doing that—otherwise I'm at your mercy.'

'I see. Well, to be honest, I'm at a bit of a loss—is it always like this?' she said suddenly, resting her elbow on the bed and propping her chin on it.

His eyes glinted. 'How do you mean?'

'Well, so far it's been a lovely blend of being friends and——' she tried to look airy '—the other.'

'This?' He lowered his hands and placed them on her hips and she gasped a little as at the same time he entered her.

His hands stilled and his eyes narrowed. 'Have I hurt you?'

'No. Oh, no. I don't think anyone's hurt me less— well, if you know what I mean, but you make me feel . . . that's so wonderful,' she said disjointedly. 'It has to be the most lovely feeling on earth——' She broke off and bit her lip.

'And that's only half of it yet—don't look like that,' he said softly and wryly. 'Most men would kill for you to be told that.' And his movements became more urgent.

It was he who made dinner in the end. After they'd showered together and he'd wrapped her carefully into her violet robe. Then he led her to the old settee in the kitchen and told her to relax.

What he made actually was bacon and eggs, his one culinary forte, he advised her, but he also fried bananas, tomato and bread, so it was a large meal and they finished it off with a lovely strong pot of coffee.

Juanita was quiet as she sipped her coffee.

'Tired?' he murmured, slipping an arm round her shoulders.

'Mmm.' She grimaced although she didn't know there were faint blue shadows beneath her eyes and she was a little pale.

'You might have done too much today,' he commented, a shade severely.

She had to smile as she laid her head on his shoulder. 'One way and another, perhaps.'

It was his turn to grimace. 'So long as there are no regrets.'

'None.' They sat in silence for a time until she said drowsily, 'You didn't tell me.'

He kissed her loose hair. 'What?'

'Whether it's always like this.'

He considered. 'We might have to wait and see,' he said eventually. 'Do you know something? Tomorrow's Saturday. Is there any hope that this place could be a haven of peace and quiet?'

'It could,' she replied, although she was still turning over in her mind what he'd said before. 'No one's coming.'

'Excellent. We can spend the next two days just as the whim takes us.'

She fingered his watch-strap. 'What about your book, though?'

'My book, thanks to you——' his voice was curiously thoughtful, she thought '—has taken a turn for the better. So much so that even two days away from it can probably only enhance it.'

'I'm so glad,' she said softly, and yawned.

'Come to bed.'

'All right. With . . . you?'

'Who else did you have in mind?'

'No one,' she protested indignantly. 'You know what I mean!'

'Don't you want to spend the night in my bed? You'd be quite safe, you know, I'm not a sex maniac——'

She sat up. 'Gareth——'

'Juanita?' he returned gravely.

She sighed. 'All right. I'd love to spend the night in your bed with you.'

'Well said! Although I must warn you that tomorrow morning could be a different story, so——'

'Take me to bed, Gareth Walker,' she commanded, 'and don't say another word.'

But, lovely as it was just to lie in his arms and feel herself drifting off to sleep, she couldn't quite make it because of her hip, which had started to ache.

'What is it?'

She told him, reluctantly, aware for the first time that she'd been unwittingly grateful that he'd made no mention of it. But all he said was, 'I'm not surprised. You *definitely* did too much today. Did you know I was an expert masseur?'

'No...'

'I've found it works well with horses. There.' He turned her away from him so he could rub her hip. 'How does that feel?'

Her eyes closed but her lips twisted. 'Other than making me feel like a horse—wonderful.' And about five minutes later she fell asleep.

Their weekend together was also wonderful although they did nothing much at all. But it was as if the unlocking of Juanita's body had unlocked her mind and they talked about all sorts of things, made love in the middle of the afternoon when it rained, swam when it was fine, listened to music and she concocted some wonderful meals.

'It's a pity it has to end,' she said on Sunday evening when they were playing Scrabble stretched out on a rug in front of a small fire they'd built in the study grate because it was raining again and chilly.

'What has to end?' he queried with a faint frown as he studied his letters.

'The peace and quiet.'

'Ah, that. Yes. For a moment I thought you had—other ideas.'

'I suppose...' she hesitated ' ... we should talk about that, though.'

He raised his eyes. 'I've got a better idea.' He paused. 'I think we should acknowledge that this state of affairs——' he put his hand over hers as she winced slightly and his gaze was very direct '—was something that, in the end, neither of us could deny.' He waited until she nodded slowly. 'And, that being the case, none of our old arguments, if you like, now apply.'

'I'm not sure what you mean,' she said uncertainly.

'I mean that a whole new world has opened up for both of us. Let's savour it a little longer, Juanita, before we try to make any decisions.'

She was silent, wondering if he meant the kind of decision that would see her become his mistress. And shivered involuntarily.

'What's wrong?'

'N-nothing...nothing,' she said hastily. 'All right. You're right, I'm sure. You're taking an awfully long time to find a word,' she pointed out.

'I've changed my mind.' He sat up and tipped his letters on to the board. 'I was beating you hollow any way——'

'You were not! I have a triple coming up with a Z in it!'

He smiled faintly. 'And I have an impulse coming up that might just scoop the pool. Have you any idea how firelight becomes you?'

Juanita stared into his eyes and recognised the look in them. She pushed her loose hair back and licked her lips but it made no difference. She experienced a sensation that began in her breasts and travelled down her body, a sensation that she knew he would, with his hands and his lips and finally his body on hers, more than triple until it became a throbbing sense of need that could only have one fulfilment.

'Gareth,' she whispered helplessly but he put a finger on her lips. Then he undressed her slowly, her fine navy jumper and hyacinth blouse and her jeans, and lingered over her beautiful French silk and lace underwear until the firelight was playing over her naked skin, gilding it and turning her nipples and areolae to rose. And he knelt up on the rug, drew her to her knees and bent his head, tasted her nipples and caressed her waist and the curve of her bottom until she shuddered with desire and tilted her head back so that her hair cascaded down like a dark, soft curtain and she made a husky, pleading little sound in her throat. His hands moved up her back then and he transferred his lips to her throat, but not for long as her body started to arch and tremble beneath his hands and finally they were together and she was parting her legs to welcome him, and accepting his weight on her with joy and urgency as they scaled a peak of pleasure together, as one, and climaxed at the same moment.

But the sheer momentousness of it left her when their bodies stilled at last and he rolled off her; she felt suddenly alone and afraid, but he pulled her into his arms as if he understood although he said nothing, and she felt his heart beating heavily and his ragged breathing, and knew that he was as moved as she was.

Yet she found herself examining that feeling of loneliness and fear the next morning, as if some small residue of it had stayed with her despite the way he'd been, and she knew that it had been a foretaste of what it would be like to live without Gareth Walker. If I'd never scaled those heights, she thought, I wouldn't know the depths... Oh, God, what should I do? she wondered.

She did nothing over the next few days but went with the flow so to speak. Which meant that they spent most of the day apart as he wrote but with none of the turbulence of before, and she supervised the transformation of his house. But they slept together, ate together, made love and spent each evening together—in effect they lived together in growing intimacy. The kind of intimacy that was much more mundane than sleeping with a man, yet just as binding.

She came to know his favourite foods and he told her about his brothers and sisters. She came to understand what a full-time occupation writing was and how draining it could be and he told her something about what went on behind the scenes with editors and agents. She found herself telling him more and more about her life and discovered that her privacy, which had become even more important to her after the accident, didn't seem to be threatened at all. He enjoyed brushing her hair for her and enjoyed watching her dress nearly as much as he enjoyed undressing her. He still massaged her hip for her every night before they fell asleep and helped her with her exercises.

And there were times when she forgot that sense of fear and the foretaste of what her life without him would be like but other times when she couldn't, although she always went out of her way to hide it from him. Such as the morning she commented on how she'd improved his early morning disposition considerably.

'Steven and Rebecca would be proud of me,' she told him as she put a breakfast tray on the bedside table and sat down on the bed. She was already dressed.

He yawned, stretched and fingered his blue-shadowed jaw. 'Why is that?'

'You're much more manageable in the mornings than you used to be.'

'Is that a fact?'

'Certainly,' she said gravely. 'Don't tell me you hadn't noticed?'

'I had noticed some things,' he agreed, his blue gaze roaming over her idly.

She raised an eyebrow. 'Such as?'

'That early mornings are particularly fine times to stay in bed and make love.'

'Only on the weekends,' she said after a moment, her lips twitching as he pulled a hand from behind his head and began to fiddle with the buttons of her blouse. He was naked from the waist up.

He replied softly, 'Don't you believe it.'

'Gareth——' she went a little pink and bit her lip '—I have a lot on today——'

'I noticed, but what goes on can always come off.' He flicked a button open.

'I didn't mean that——' She stared at him frustratedly, noting the entirely wicked glint in his eyes. 'I mean I'm all set and ready to go,' she tried to explain.

His teeth glinted in a particularly devilish grin. 'So am I, so am I,' he murmured.

'Oh! You're impossible...'

He laughed outright then and pulled her into his arms. 'And I was right about you,' he said when he'd finished kissing her. 'You're one of those impossibly bright, early morning people. Well, so be it.' And he moved her away from him, straightened her blouse and smoothed her hair.

She muttered something incomprehensible and, to her dismay, discovered she didn't feel like going anywhere.

'What now?' he queried.

She sighed. 'I've just got the feeling you've ruined my day.'

He pushed his hair off his forehead and looked at her wryly. 'That could make two of us but, seeing as I was trying to be strong, not to mention altogether reformed, perhaps it would be character-building to let me continue with it.'

She digested this, her expression ranging from severity to rueful humour finally. 'I think you were having me on all along—— Oh, no——' she twisted away as he reached for her '—I'm all for building character, Mr Walker. I shall see you this evening!' And she fled the room laughing but only moments later discovered her laughter turning to tears...

'The kids will be home tomorrow.'

'Yes.'

They were eating dinner in the kitchen—spaghetti bolognese and salad—and there was an open bottle of red wine between them, and the long weekend stretched behind Juanita, filled with memories that she knew would stay with her for the rest of her life but also that growing sense of fear.

She took a sudden breath. 'Gareth? What will we do? I can't just go on like this—I'm *sorry*,' she said intensely. 'But the longer it does go on, the harder it will be to... you were right about that. And I can't visualise myself as—well, as a mistress. Perhaps if there were no children involved or—but even then... You see, I thought I could do it because, well, we talked about hope once. But I know now I can't.'

'Only now?' he queried very quietly.

She wound some spaghetti round and round her fork. 'No.' She blinked and rubbed her nose with the back of her hand. 'I've tried to hide it but it's been growing. I think it's best if I...go forward from this with confidence and...whatever rather than stay and become bitter. But don't think I blame you. I knew.'

'Go forward to some other man making love to you?' She flinched and closed her eyes.

'Juanita?'

'Don't,' she whispered.

'But I'm interested.'

'No, you're just being cruel,' she said hoarsely.

'Not really. I have another plan, you see, which rather depends on whether you can see yourself in anyone else's arms, doing the things you do—to me.'

Her lashes lifted and she couldn't hide the pain in her eyes. 'Why? What plan? I've just told you what would happen to me but you *knew* anyway. It's the way I'm made, it's to do with my parents and all that. But even more it's to do with *me*. There's always going to be one lack in my life so if I can't ever find a full, loving relationship—and I may *never*, but to try to substitute it with something less would be—what do they say about two wrongs?' Her eyes were full of tears now but she made no effort to hide them.

'Juanita——' his eyes were sombre and deadly serious '—what I'm trying to find out is, if you believe you love me and could put up with me for the rest of our lives, I think we should get married.'

Her mouth fell open and stayed open until she suddenly sprang up feverishly. 'No. N-no,' she gasped. 'I c-couldn't. I...I...' But her stammer wouldn't let her continue and then something really strange happened to her. All the blood seemed to drain from her head to her feet and everything went black.

'Gareth...?'

'Mmm?' He was bending over her, his eyes dark with anxiety and she was sitting propped up on the settee.

'What happened?'

He sighed and sat down beside her and started to massage her hands. 'You fainted. Right after I suggested we get married.'

Her brow creased. 'But why?'

He looked at her carefully, noting the returning colour to her cheeks, then said, 'I was hoping you could tell me that. I assumed it came as such a shock——' He shrugged.

'It did,' Juanita agreed huskily and started to look agitated again.

'No, hang on,' he ordered and picked up a glass of brandy from the floor. 'Have some of this.' He waited until she'd taken a few sips. 'You told me once you're not the fainting type. But is there any other reason it could have been? Healthwise, I mean?'

'No! I'm fine.'

'You've been doing an awful lot this week,' he said slowly. 'And I mean a lot of work. Acting as unpaid wallpaper-hanger to mention just one instance.'

'That's . . . that's because all this has been building up in me,' she whispered.

'I might have known,' he commented and his voice was dry. 'Which was all my fault. Look, do you remember what I said about this being a whole new ball game or words to that effect, Juanita?'

She moistened her lips. 'W-well, yes.'

'That doesn't tell me whether you agree or not.'

'I suppose in some ways it has to,' she said cautiously.

'Then I'll tell you one way that it has. I can't visualise this house and my life without you now. I can't visualise my bed without you. So. . .' he paused and his gaze was so compelling that she couldn't tear hers away '. . .things have changed for me. Which is not to say that I will ever be the ideal husband for anyone, nor does it automatically discount the possibility that you might be able or perhaps want to go forward from this with confidence and find someone who is—but if not, will you marry me, Juanita?'

She opened her mouth several times but finally it came out quite plainly and starkly. 'You could just be feeling sorry for me.'

'Have I ever shown you that I felt sorry for you? Has it restrained me from mocking you at times, not to mention being quite rude and overbearing? Have I ever, in other words, treated you any differently from how I treat everyone else?'

'No,' she said slowly. 'I . . . it's still only been a matter of weeks!'

He smiled but it didn't reach his eyes. 'What happened to us happened in a matter of hours, Juanita. The only thing that's changed is that it's got stronger and stronger.'

She reached out and took the glass of brandy from him and took a gulp this time. 'Don't you think, though, that if you've changed enough to want to marry again it could become a frustration not to be able to have children? You're so good with them,' she said unhappily.

'I think,' he said slowly, 'the only regrets I'll have will be on your behalf. And it's not so much that I've changed simply to want marriage for the sake of it, I want *you*.'

She blushed and trembled at the look in his eyes. 'That could change,' she whispered.

'It might,' he conceded and his lips twisted at the unwittingly crestfallen look that came to her eyes. 'I mean, it may get to the stage where I can control myself better, but what I can't see changing is the sense of peace you bring to me.'

'Do I?' Her eyes widened.

'I thought you might have noticed?'

'Well . . . oh, I don't know what to say or do.' She twisted her hands.

'You haven't told me whether you could see yourself making love to any other man.'

'No. . .' It was out before she could stop herself and there was an anguished ring to it that was unmistakable; and he did smile at last, with his eyes and right into hers.

'Well, then,' he murmured in the moment before he took her into his arms, 'I think that settles it.'

CHAPTER TEN

JUANITA drove to Sydney two days later, not sure if she was on her head or her heels and with a beautiful sapphire in an old-fashioned setting on her left hand. It was Gareth's mother's ring, and when she'd been unable to stop herself from asking if it had also been his first wife's he'd told her that his mother had still been alive when he'd first married. And he'd taken her into his study, unlocked a drawer and shown her the photos she'd missed about the house of his tragic first wife, and his son, an enchanting-looking child who'd died just before his first birthday and resembled his father.

'Why do you lock them away?' she'd asked awkwardly. 'Are the memories still so painful?'

'No. Contrary to what one wants to believe, time is a great healer. It—was an era of my life I'm not terribly proud of; perhaps that's why. But I do visit their graves.'

'Don't stop because of me,' she'd warned, and sniffed, concentrating on his first wife, Linda. 'She was beautiful,' she'd said at last.

'Yes.' That was all he'd said, but after he'd packed it all away again he'd taken her hand and raised it to his lips, and she'd felt curiously reassured by this small gesture.

But when he'd insisted they break the news to Wendy and the twins as soon as they arrived back, she'd experienced a moment of panic, despite their obvious delight and Rebecca's voicing of a sentiment that took both her and Gareth by surprise. 'I knew it,' she'd said.

'Knew what?' Gareth had enquired.

'I just had a feeling about you two!'

'Did you indeed?' he'd murmured.

'You did not!' Steven had protested. 'You didn't say anything.' He'd looked at her aggrievedly.

'Boys don't understand these things as well as girls do,' his twin sister had replied loftily.

'I must say, I...well, I hoped something like this might happen,' Wendy had then confided, causing Steven to look even further put out, so much so that Gareth had taken pity on him.

'I've got the feeling, young man, that you and I are going to need each other for moral support—we're in danger of being overrun by women.' And he'd put his arm round Steven's shoulders, to the little boy's obvious delight.

'Would you like me to come with you?'

'No,' Juanita had said the night before she'd left. 'Gareth—well, a lot of it will be business, I should have gone up to town days ago. The curtains and bedspreads are nearly ready and I want to make sure they're just right. I'm *not* happy with one set of wallpaper I chose so I'm going to see if I can change it, and your book's going so well——'

'It is, but what about your parents?'

She'd quietened and thought of that moment of panic she'd experienced when he'd told the kids, and was able suddenly to find its root. Did she believe Gareth Walker really loved her, or did she believe it was more compassion and guilt because she'd been unable to hide what she felt for him? And if so should she have allowed him to insist on marrying her...? Which was why, she'd seen, making it all public worried her, to put it mildly.

She'd said at last, 'Would you mind if I told them first?'

'Do you think they're likely to disapprove?'

She'd swallowed and managed to smile. 'The opposite if anything. You could find yourself almost embarrassed by their enthusiasm.'

'I doubt it—not having second thoughts by any chance, Juanita?' He'd tilted her chin and stared into her eyes.

'What would you say if I were?' she'd whispered.

He'd been silent for a moment, then, 'I don't think I'd say anything. There are other, much more effective ways of showing you how much we—need each other.'

Her lips had trembled, her whole body in fact had trembled, and was only stilled when he drew her into his arms. 'Remember this,' he'd said into her hair.

How could I forget it? she asked herself as she steered her car up the Hume Highway. It doesn't solve my dilemma, though. Did I let myself be railroaded into this? she asked herself helplessly.

But an hour or so later a chain of events was begun that had incredible consequences. She drove straight to Bluemoon and was giving a report to her superior when once again she fainted mid-sentence.

Which saw her the following afternoon in her specialist's surgery at her mother's insistence after a confused day of tests and then more tests and an uncomfortable night wondering what was wrong with her and being cosseted by her maternal parent. Her father was in Adelaide, apparently, with Damien, for the Grand Prix. Her only other cause for thanks was that she'd had the foresight to remove her engagement-ring before entering the Bluemoon offices, so she'd not had that to explain. She'd also warded off her mother's intention to accompany her to this consultation——

Something else to give thanks for as she said, '*What*?'

Her specialist eyed her from the other side of his desk. 'Juanita, I can't tell you how happy I am for you.'

She put her hand to her head extremely dazedly. 'But you told me this couldn't happen!'

'My dear, we told you it was *extremely* unlikely in view of certain damage caused by the accident. But the body is a wonderful thing and is given to healing itself a lot more than we give it credit for. I must admit, though, at the time—well, perhaps I let myself forget it, although I shouldn't have. We've all seen cases of women who can't seem to conceive for a variety of reasons, but once they adopt a child and stop worrying about it, bingo, as they say. And there appears at this although extremely early stage to be no reason why this pregnancy shouldn't come to term quite normally, although we'd like to monitor it as closely as possible, of course.'

'Of course,' she echoed hollowly. 'Oh, my God!'

He frowned. 'Juanita——'

'No——' she swallowed '—it's all my fault. I just—I just lacked faith, I suppose!'

'That's not so hard to understand after what you went through and what we told you,' he said quietly and kindly. 'It's also an area that's so closely bound up with one's innate feelings about oneself, one's femininity or masculinity as the case may be.'

She stared at him and knew he was about to ask her about this baby's father so she said hastily, 'But why does it make me faint?'

'Ah. I don't think the two things are connected. You appear to be a bit anaemic, which of course we'll have to do something about, and if you've been over working——'

'Do you mean, you only came across this—pregnancy by accident?'

'You could say so.'

*   *   *

'Juanita, please darling, stop!'

Juanita moved convulsively and sat up. 'Mum, will you just go away?' Her face was tear-streaked and swollen, her hair awry and her clothes crumpled.

'*No,*' her mother said decisively. 'You told me you were fine and then you came in here and you've been crying ever since. Now I know there are some things you feel you can never forgive me for but to take it out on me like this is...is...'

Juanita took a breath. 'I'm not! Oh, Mum, don't think that.'

Her mother sat down opposite her on the bed. 'Then what is it, darling?'

'You're never going to believe this, Mum, but I'm...I'm pregnant.'

'My dear, my...' Her mother went no further. Instead she simply opened her arms and Juanita flew into them.

And it was a good five minutes before her mother said, still sounding dazed but happy, 'Who is he—the father? Is there a problem? Why aren't you just over the moon?' She sobered suddenly. 'Tell me, love.'

And, to her amazement, Juanita found herself telling her almost everything, although she omitted any reference that would identify Gareth.

'But I don't understand—he wants to marry you and——'

'Mum,' Juanita said wearily, 'for the life of me, before this I didn't know whether it was as much that he felt sorry for me and guilty about me. But one thing I do know—children are just not on his agenda. I told you why and the incredible irony is that perhaps I could have made it work the way I was, or assumed I was—I think I must have always had that hope in my heart and that's why I gave in, in spite of my doubts. But this...this is like trapping him,' she said with fresh tears streaming down her face.

'Well, in the meantime, what will we do?'

Juanita drank the tea her mother had brought her. 'Would you mind telling a little white lie for me?'

'To...?'

'No, to Bluemoon. Just that I'm not very well and need a short break. Nothing serious—tell them I'm anaemic, which is true. Fortunately I'd just about finished a progress report when I fainted, so somebody—and they'll just have to *find* somebody—should be able to supervise things without too much trouble.'

'But——'

'Mum, I just need a couple of days to *think*.'

'I'm all for that—Juanita, is this job anyway linked to this man?'

'Why do you say that?' Juanita asked quickly, too quickly perhaps.

'You've been away so much—it just crossed my mind.'

Juanita was silent then she nodded briefly.

'So it's Gareth Walker?'

'Mum...' She said it pleadingly.

'It's all right,' her mother replied reassuringly. 'I'm not going to beard him in his den or *tell* anyone, although I have met him,' she said thoughtfully. 'But had you considered that if someone else descends on his doorstep he might come looking for you?'

'I'm...considering it right now. Mum...it's *my* prerogative to tell him about this baby, or not to.'

'Of course, darling.'

'Do you swear?'

'Cross my heart.' Her mother smiled faintly for the first time but she added, 'Just promise me one thing. Do just that—think about it for a few days before you make any decisions. In the meantime I'll hold the whole world at bay if necessary.'

Why can't I think? Juanita asked herself that night. Why can't I say to myself, You've got three options: have this baby on my own or not have it—I couldn't do that—or tell Gareth...?

Come on, she commanded herself. Start with number one: have this baby on your own. Do you think he'd let you do that? He can't force you to the altar, although... Go away and have it so he doesn't know?

She shivered but the thought began to take hold. I must have a few months up my sleeve before it's noticeable, quite a few, so—but how to break it all off? I could tell him the truth—that I just don't believe it's a complete relationship so I've decided to end it—but I'd have to write and then I'd have to... put myself out of his reach for a while in case he did try to make me change my mind. Which means I'd probably have to say goodbye to Bluemoon and my job; but why doesn't that seem so important any longer?

'Because I'm going to have a baby,' she whispered aloud in the darkness. 'I don't think it's really hit me yet but I'm going to be normal—surely that must compensate a bit for—losing Gareth?'

It was the next morning when Juanita, still with nothing resolved in her mind, and her mother got the news that Damien had crashed his car in a practice run for the Adelaide Grand Prix and had been rushed to hospital in a critical condition.

'I don't believe it,' her mother moaned. 'Both my children——'

Juanita held her. 'But this one survived; remember that.' And they flew to Adelaide on the first available flight. It was of course no real coincidence that they should bump into Xanthe at Adelaide Airport—she had just disembarked from a flight from Perth.

And there was no mistaking her white-faced anguish as she ran up to Juanita. 'Oh, thank God,' she said tearfully. 'I was thinking of disguising myself as a nurse because I didn't think they'd let me see him otherwise, but I can come with you, can't I? *Please*, Juanita.'

In fact no one saw Damien for hours as he underwent complicated surgery, a process that was particularly trying for Juanita with all the memories it aroused—and that was where Xanthe came into her own. If I'd suspected her of being a pillar of strength at a time like this I would have wondered if I was losing my mind, she mused, watching the other girl holding her mother's hand while she spoke to her gently and reassuringly, but that's just what she is. Even Dad has taken to her, although he looks at her now and then as if to say, Have I met you before? But what will Damien say when he sees her? If he sees her...

Damien in fact held out his hand from his bed very late that night after a successful operation and said with a palpable effort, 'Xanthe? Is it really you? I've missed you so much...'

'Well!' The Spencer-Hill seniors looked at each other bemusedly, then at Juanita. They'd left Xanthe and Damien alone—there might as well have been no one else in the room anyway.

Juanita grimaced and explained. 'Who knows?' she finished. 'They might just be the right ones for each other, but heaven alone knows what Gareth—er—what her brother will think.'

Her mother blinked then said bewilderedly, 'I may be wrong but I think he's standing right behind you, darling—she did say she was Gareth Walker's sister, you see.'

Juanita thought she might faint again but she didn't. In fact as she turned slowly a tidal wave of colour coursed up from the base of her throat.

He looked tired and crumpled and as if the tweed jacket he wore over his khaki shirt and jeans was only an afterthought. But as they stared at each other and his gaze wandered from her flushed cheeks down to her bare left hand, then back to her eyes, his eyes were very blue but cold and angry.

'You've come about Xanthe, of course,' she said foolishly. 'I——'

'No. This time Xanthe's on her own,' he said grimly. 'I've come about you.'

'I——'

But her mother was galvanised into action. 'We'll leave you to it,' she said brightly. 'Come along, dear!'

'But I don't understand,' Juanita's father said. 'First a girl I've never met commandeers my son and now a complete stranger who is apparently her brother commandeers my——'

'Come *along*, dear——'

'No,' Gareth said again, more pleasantly—but only just—as he turned to them. 'I do apologise for, as you put it, "commandeering" your daughter, sir, but the fact of the matter is that I plan to marry her and, much as I would like to meet you before I do, perhaps tomorrow morning would be a better time for that. In the meantime, Juanita and I have a few things to discuss but I thought my hotel might be a more convivial spot for *that*; she looks out on her feet.'

'Of all the—what makes you think you can treat my mother and father like that?' she said tensely as he helped her into a taxi. There had appeared little option but to go with him, particularly in face of her mother's serious look and nod of her head.

'I'm not marrying them, I'm marrying you,' he replied laconically, and added to the driver, 'Take us to whatever your best hotel is, mate. I get them confused from city to city.'

'You haven't even *got* a hotel!'

'Don't split hairs, Juanita,' he drawled.

'I...I...' she spluttered, then said coldly, 'I'm not. This city is in the grip of Grand Prix fever, don't forget.'

He swore then shrugged. 'We'll see.'

Whereupon at one of the city's plushest hotels she was treated to a display of Gareth Walker at his dazzling best and, although for a staggering sum, they were soon being ushered almost with reverence to a suite that overlooked Adelaide, city of churches and motor races. The fact that neither of them had any luggage apart from the briefcase Gareth carried appeared to be of no concern to anyone.

The fact that he registered her quite audibly under her own name and as his fiancée, on the other hand, stopped a couple of what turned out to be journalists passing by in their tracks, one with a camera, and as they were handed into the lift she was not only photographed with Gareth's arm about her but besieged with questions about her engagement and for news of her brother.

She was shaking with anger when the door of the suite finally closed on them. 'You can't just do this to me,' she said whitely.

'Why not? I thought you agreed to it.' He opened the mini-bar and started to pour two drinks.

'Y-you...you must know I've changed my mind,' she said shakily.

'Do I?' He strolled over to her and put a glass in her hand. 'I'll tell you what I know. That I've had no word from you since you left and no reply from your apartment, which I thought was strange. Then I tried Bluemoon this afternoon to be greeted with news that you'd been taken ill and someone else would be taking over but that they were unable to put me in touch with you because, according to your mother, you were not to be contacted for several days at least. That was when,' he said grimly, 'I jumped in the car and drove to Sydney. And one way or another I have been driving and flying around the country ever since.'

'You...must have heard about Damien,' she whispered.

'Yes, on my car radio in between searching Lavender Bay, Woollahra where your mother lives and the North Shore where your father and brother have their home bases. That's when I changed direction and my mode of transport.'

She closed her eyes. 'I'm sorry. I was going to try to explain but when this came up...' She gestured and spilt some drink so she put the glass down carefully.

'Explain what?' he queried, still in that hard voice.

'Why I can't marry you...'

'Tell me one thing first. Are you sick or was that an excuse?'

She bit her lip. 'A bit anaemic, that's all, nothing serious.'

'All right.' His gaze roamed over her and she tensed and made an involuntary movement that would have been a dead give-away had she not caught herself. Even so his eyes narrowed as he murmured, 'Go ahead.'

And she said in a fluster of sudden fright curiously mixed with a surge of anger, 'N-no, Gareth, I don't have to explain anything. I have changed my mind, it's as simple as that.'

'Because of anything your mother and father have come up with? Your father didn't even appear to know.'

'He didn't——'

'But your mother seemed to think you should come with me so she's obviously not totally in the dark.'

Juanita took a breath. 'She knows,' she said distraughtly then, 'but——'

'And what objection does she have?' he shot at her.

'She d-doesn't——'

'So?'

She stiffened. 'Don't do this to me—what right have you to treat me like this? As if I'm a prisoner in a dock—why would I want to marry you anyway when you can be like this——?'

'Because,' he said silkily, 'you love me, but in lieu of any other explanation, and, like a typical woman, have either convinced yourself that you don't or that I don't——'

'No, you don't!' she all but shouted at him. 'You were the one who told me you never planned to marry again; you are the one who's never actually said you love me; you were the one who said the only regret you would have if we didn't have children would be——' She stopped abruptly.

'Would be,' he said slowly, 'on your behalf. Why does that upset you so much, Juanita?'

She stared at him through her tears and then her shoulders slumped with the knowledge that she couldn't hide from him forever; he had a right to know if nothing else and then perhaps he would understand. 'The impossible has happened,' she said huskily and wearily.

He took a suddenly indrawn breath and moved his hands.

She said, 'I don't know if you can believe this but I genuinely thought it couldn't—I've lived my life since the accident on that premise, you could say; the way I am, or rather was, was all because of it, but it seems my body was quietly going around healing itself, and now it's making a baby—I can't help thinking it's the supreme way of showing me how I lacked faith, wouldn't you agree?'

'No,' he said very quietly and took her hand, 'I think it's much more simple. I think your body is fulfilling our love, that's all.'

'But——'

'Look,' he said, 'before you say anything else, do one thing for me—sit down and read this.'

'Read what?' she said bewilderedly.

'It's the summary of my book, the kind of thing I'd send to my editor—I took your advice.'

Juanita stared at him. 'About writing out your dilemma with literature—what has that to do with this?'

'About writing out my dilemma but not with literature with a capital L or otherwise. You'll see.' He released her hand and reached for his briefcase.

It took several minutes before she was able to concentrate on the typescript he handed her. But then the words unblurred and began to make sense and what she read was about a man who could have been Gareth...

'It's you,' she said dazedly, 'but...'

'Yes. Read on. It explains some things.'

She read. Then she lifted her head and stared at him with her lips parted. 'Is th-this t-true?' she stammered.

He sat down opposite her. 'All too true. But, being something of a fool, I had to set it down on paper to sort it out. You see, Juanita, I had thought I could live the rest of my life more or less alone. I thought that was how I was made and I was going along quite well until you knocked at my door. I even had a ready-made family at my disposal, in Wendy and the twins—something you noted, if you recall. I had the freedom I thought was so important to me and I could never visualise willingly putting myself in a situation like my last marriage, where she was torn and I was torn by a lack of independence, but I escaped most of it and she escaped—nothing. But from the moment you came into my life all those things I thought I prized began to lose their meaning. You, in fact, were the one to spot it first.'

'How...wh-when...?' she stammered.

He smiled briefly. 'One night at the kitchen table. Don't you remember telling me I could be lacking some permanence in my life?'

Juanita's lips parted. 'But you didn't see it then.'

'No,' he agreed. 'Although it had already begun to manifest itself.'

'How?'

'I couldn't settle to anything, least of all writing. But I was convinced it was writer's block and then I tried to lay it all at Laura Hennessey's door.' He smiled drily. 'And more and more I was feeling guilty about you.'

Juanita took a joltingly little breath but he said before she could speak, 'Because I wanted you more and more, and no amount of telling myself I wasn't a fit—mate for you changed that. But then I could no longer ignore...what I was doing to you, and perhaps because my whole concept of myself was based on guilt anyway I—did what I did.'

They stared at each other until Juanita looked down at the typescript in her hands. 'So you wrote about a man going through the same thing—all the time we were...' She stopped.

He smiled unexpectedly. 'Living together? Yes. I wrote, according to my editor—he came to see me the day you left—better than I've ever done, although he didn't see the—crucial bits.'

'Booker Prize stuff?' she asked, her eyes wide.

He took the typescript from her and put it aside, then took her hand. 'I doubt it; anyway it will never be published——'

'Oh! But——'

'No,' he said quietly but quite definitely. 'Because it's something intensely private; it's only between you and me——'

'But your editor...'

His lips twisted. 'Is tearing his hair out, but I told him he'd have to live in the hope that my new...insights would prompt me to be a better writer. You see, my darling Juanita,' he said steadily but with a curious note in his voice, 'as I wrote I began to understand about the guilt. And understand that I'd never before been able to set apart the tragic way they died from the reality of my relationship with Linda.

'Because the truth is neither of us was ready for marriage and children—we might never have been with each other. It was a relationship that most probably wouldn't have succeeded even in ideal circumstances because the commitment you have with someone you love ultimately wasn't there. We were two rather trendy people who lived rather lonely lives because of our professions, and we just didn't see that our hunger for independence wasn't part of the new order—husbands and wives who did their own things—but a lack of true, binding love.

'Only I couldn't really see—I couldn't dissociate it from the tragedy that ended it, and the guilt, until I started to write about it. And then the blinkers seemed to fall off and I began to understand. I began to see that I wasn't a leopard who couldn't change his spots—just a man who had never properly loved before.'

'Gareth——'

But he stilled the urgent movement she made and put his other hand around hers. 'Before you say anything, I've lived today in a frenzy of fear and desperation. Fear that there was something seriously wrong with you and desperation that I might not be able to find you and show you this as well as tell you that I *love* you, that I'm hopeless without you—and tell you now that should you want to have ten children it's fine with me. Because *this* news, instead of filling me with foreboding, has done the opposite. Unfortunately,' he said with a wry little glint and then he sobered again.

'What do you mean?' She stared at him.

He released her hand and placed his very gently on her stomach. 'I meant that if I thought I loved you and was fascinated before, I'm now having even greater trouble keeping my hands off you.'

She flushed faintly. 'So you do believe I was quite sure it couldn't happen?'

'Not only that but I'm having difficulty *not* believing it was all somehow my doing.'

'Well, it was. I mean . . . part of it was.' She blushed quite hotly this time and his lips twitched.

But he took both her hands in his again and said in a more serious tone, 'What do I have to do to convince you that this wonderful news for you, my love, is also the best news of my life? I've talked a lot about—other things, *my* life, my this, my that, but perhaps I've missed the most important thing. You. None of this could have happened to me otherwise. I just, despite my best efforts and despite the opposition you tried to conjure up, fell in love with *you*. Right from the beginning,' he said. 'You unsettled me the moment I laid eyes on you and it never changed. You were unusual and stunning and at times so still—like the portrait I thought your mother should have painted, but then there was the fire in your eyes when I made you angry. It was as if everything about you spoke to my senses.'

He shook his head and she could see something like wonder in his eyes, and it made her tremble and remember how, that first day, she'd experienced the same thing.

He went on, 'You were such an enigma *I* used to wonder at times if I'd ever understand you. And if I'd thought you were stunning when we first met—I'll never forget the day you came to me wearing a jumper that matched your lipstick, a sort of deep berry colour, and it was like a symphony for me—your skin, your hair, this wonderful colour—but you were so cool...

'I really wanted, that morning, to undress you so there would only be the colour on your lips—I had the greatest difficulty preventing myself,' he said barely audibly, his eyes resting on her lips then roaming to her hair.

A couple of tears sparkled on her lashes but they were tears of joy now, because she could no longer doubt that these were the words of a man as fascinated with her as she was with him, a man to whom her limp and stammer had truly meant nothing. 'I wish I'd known,' she said gravely, 'and I seriously deny conjuring Laura Hennessey up. But——' her lips dimpled at the corners '—I do think ten children might be a bit excessive.'

If she'd had any lingering doubts they were swept away by the convulsive movement he made, and she had to acknowledge that she knew Gareth Walker well enough now to know that he was deeply moved. 'I love you,' she said softly and took her hand back, but only to slip it under her blouse and bring out his ring, worn on a chain. 'I couldn't bring myself to part with it entirely.'

'Juanita——'

But she put a finger to his lips. 'You said once you wouldn't have to tell me how we needed each other, you would only have to show me.'

'So I did.' And with unsteady fingers he undid the buttons of her blouse and took it off, then her bra, and stared down at his ring which was nestled between her breasts. Then he lifted his eyes to hers, and they were very bright as he said unsteadily, 'Do you know how that makes me feel? As if I've come home after years of roaming in a wilderness.'

It was her turn to be moved almost beyond bearing, but he took her in his arms at last and said in the moment before he kissed her, 'Don't ever leave me again.'

Hi!
I should be on cloud
nine. Rolf Felder asked
me to marry him. He's
the handsome owner of
a hotel chain here in
Switzerland, but I'm
not convinced he'll ever
view our marriage as
anything more than one
of convenience. I'm
desperately in love
with him—*what should
I do?*   Love, Abigail

Relive the romance.... This December,
Harlequin and Silhouette are proud to bring you

by Request™

Little Matchmakers

All they want for Christmas is a mom *and* a dad!

Three complete novels by your favorite authors—
in one special collection!

THE MATCHMAKERS by Debbie Macomber
MRS. SCROOGE by Barbara Bretton
A CAROL CHRISTMAS by Muriel Jensen

When your child's a determined little matchmaker,
anything can happen—especially at Christmas!

Available wherever
Harlequin and Silhouette books are sold.

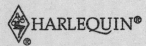

HARLEQUIN® **Silhouette®**

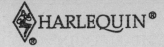

EDGE OF ETERNITY
Jasmine Cresswell

Two years after their divorce, David Powell
and Eve Graham met again in Eternity,
Massachusetts—and this time there was magic
between them. But David was tied up in a
murder that no amount of small-town gossip
could free him from. When Eve was pulled into
the frenzy, he knew he had to come up with
some answers—including how to convince her
they should marry again...this time for keeps.

EDGE OF ETERNITY, available in
November from Intrigue, is the sixth book in
Harlequin's exciting new cross-line series,
WEDDINGS, INC.

Be sure to look for the final book, **VOWS,** by
Margaret Moore (Harlequin Historical #248),
coming in December.